AF279287

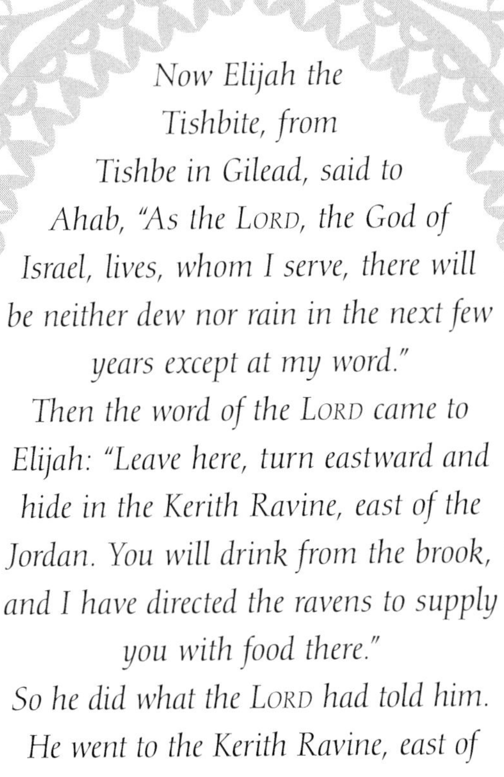

*Now Elijah the
Tishbite, from
Tishbe in Gilead, said to
Ahab, "As the LORD, the God of
Israel, lives, whom I serve, there will
be neither dew nor rain in the next few
years except at my word."
Then the word of the LORD came to
Elijah: "Leave here, turn eastward and
hide in the Kerith Ravine, east of the
Jordan. You will drink from the brook,
and I have directed the ravens to supply
you with food there."
So he did what the LORD had told him.
He went to the Kerith Ravine, east of*

the Jordan, and stayed there. The ravens brought him bread and meat in the morning and bread and meat in the evening, and he drank from the brook. Some time later the brook dried up because there had been no rain in the land. Then the word of the LORD came to him: "Go at once to Zarephath in the region of Sidon and stay there. I have directed a widow there to supply you with food." So he went to Zarephath. When he came to the town gate, a widow was there gathering sticks. He called to her and asked, "Would you bring me a little water in a jar so I may have a drink?" As she was going to get it, he called, "And bring me, please, a piece of bread."

"As surely as the LORD your God lives," she replied, "I don't have any bread—only a handful

*of flour in a jar and a little olive oil in a jug.
I am gathering a few sticks to take home and
make a meal for myself and my son, that
we may eat it—and die."*
*Elijah said to her, "Don't be afraid. Go home and
do as you have said. But first make a small loaf
of bread for me from what you have and bring it
to me, and then make something for yourself and
your son. For this is what the* Lord, *the God of
Israel, says: 'The jar of flour will not be used up
and the jug of oil will not run dry until the day
the* Lord *sends rain on the land.'"*
*She went away and did as Elijah had told her.
So there was food every day for Elijah and for
the woman and her family. For the jar of flour
was not used up and the jug of oil did not run*

*dry, in keeping with the word of the
L*ORD* spoken by Elijah.
Some time later the son of the woman who owned
the house became ill. He grew worse and worse, and
finally stopped breathing. She said to Elijah, "What
do you have against me, man of God? Did you
come to remind me of my sin and kill my son?"
"Give me your son," Elijah replied. He took him
from her arms, carried him to the upper room
where he was staying, and laid him on his
bed. Then he cried out to the L*ORD, "L*ORD* my
God, have you brought tragedy even on this
widow I am staying with, by causing her son to
die?" Then he stretched himself out on the boy
three times and cried out to the L*ORD, "L*ORD* my
God, let this boy's life return to him!"*

*The LORD heard Elijah's cry, and the boy's life returned to him, and he lived. Elijah picked up the child and carried him down from the room into the house. He gave him to his mother and said, "Look, your son is alive!"*
*Then the woman said to Elijah, "Now I know that you are a man of God and that the word of the LORD from your mouth is the truth."*

—1 KINGS 17 (NIV)

*Ordinary Women* of the BIBLE

✦

A MOTHER'S SACRIFICE: JOCHEBED'S STORY
THE HEALER'S TOUCH: TIKVA'S STORY
THE ARK BUILDER'S WIFE: ZARAH'S STORY
AN UNLIKELY WITNESS: JOANNA'S STORY
THE LAST DROP OF OIL: ADALIAH'S STORY

*Ordinary Women* of the BIBLE

# THE LAST DROP OF OIL

## ADALIAH'S STORY

VIRGINIA SMITH

# THE LAST DROP OF OIL

## ADALIAH'S STORY

For my mom, Amy Barkman.

May your oil jug never go dry.

—Ginny

# CHAPTER ONE

**D**awn broke before Adaliah was ready. The lightening eastern sky crept over the dark silhouette of the distant hills with surprising speed. She fumbled with the rope as she pulled the jug from the depths of the well. Itthobaal would be awake, dressed, and waiting for her when she returned to their house. An image of his face—eyes narrowed with impatience, lips drawn tight—rose before her, and she nearly lost her grip on the rope.

"Pay attention," the woman next to her snapped. Her arm shot out to grab the rope before the jug fell back into the well. "You'll break the jug with your clumsiness."

Adaliah kept her gaze on the woman's hands, but from the corner of her eye she saw the smirk the woman turned on the others who waited their turn to draw water.

"Maybe that's her aim." The second in line wore a blue scarf over her dark hair. Her voice took on a sneer. "Then her husband could sell the village a new one at a fat profit."

"No, Keprea, the new well jug would come from your husband's kiln." Though the first woman spoke to her friend, her taunting gaze remained fixed on Adaliah. "Why give profit to the husband of one so inept at the simplest of tasks, like drawing water?"

The barb struck home, and Adaliah shut her eyes against the sting. Inept. The word was one she heard often at home. Her cooking was inferior to that of Itthobaal's first wife. Her stitching was not as fine. Adaliah's patch of garden produced an inadequate harvest in comparison to the bounty of Maresheh's. If Adaliah had dared to argue, she could have pointed out that the drought that gripped the land had squeezed every drop of life from any vegetables she might have been able to coax from the dry soil. But an argument would only earn her a slap, so she held her tongue. Besides, it might launch another long tribute to the incomparable merits of his first wife.

Indeed, Maresheh must have had the blood of gods running through her veins, for every task she performed had been done to perfection, according to Itthobaal and his daughter.

*Every task except the most important.* A satisfied warmth flooded her at the thought of Danel, the beautiful son she had born Itthobaal four years ago.

Aware that the women watched her closely, Adaliah kept her face a stoic mask. She hauled the clay jug over the lip of the well and filled her jar with clear, fresh water, then set the jug down on the stone with excessive care. Without meeting anyone's eye, she hefted her container to her shoulder and left the well. The murmur of their whispers faded behind her.

A western breeze carried the salty scent of the Great Sea through the nearly silent village. An increasing glow behind the hills illuminated the horizon, but the sun's fingers had yet to spread into the sky. Perhaps fortune would be with her and Itthobaal would not yet have emerged from the bedchamber they shared. She might yet be able to assemble the morning meal of bread, olives, and cheese before he became aware of her lateness. She increased her pace, careful not to slosh precious water from the jar, her sandals kicking up dust on the village's main street.

When she rounded the corner, her hopes shrank. The curtain on the ground floor window of Itthobaal's house stood open, and the light of a lamp flickered inside. An invisible hand constricted her stomach. He had awakened, and she had not been there with his morning meal.

Steeling herself with a deep breath, she pushed open the door.

*"Imma!"*

Her son flung himself toward her, arms thrown wide. Adaliah braced herself in the seconds before he crashed into her and wrapped her legs in a fierce hug. Even so, water sloshed over the rim of the jar and spilled down her back.

"Watch out, woman," Itthobaal growled from across the room. "That's one of my finest pieces. If you break it…"

He left the threat hanging, and Adaliah had no trouble filling the gap. In the almost five years since her wedding she'd learned what could happen when she angered Itthobaal.

Danel released her and threw his head back to fix dark eyes on her face. "I woke up, and I looked for you."

"I was at the well. The task took longer than expected," she told the child, with a glance toward her husband. "There was a crowd at the well."

His nostril curled in a sneer. "Get there earlier tomorrow."

Nodding, she disengaged herself from Danel and unwrapped her linen scarf from her head and neck. When it hung on its peg by the door, she hurried to the sturdy worktable in the corner. If the only punishment for her tardiness was a scolding, Itthobaal was in a good mood. That boded well for the day.

She filled two cups with the milk she had gotten from their goat before her trip to the well and set them on the thick mat that served as their table. Both Itthobaal and Danel sank onto their cushions. Itthobaal raised his cup as she hurried to assemble the rest of the meal.

"Do you see this, boy?" He held the item aloft between them. "That's fine work at the wheel. Some men think all they have to do is slap on a lump of clay and give the wheel a few kicks. But a piece like this takes skill. Look how thin the sides are, and not a flaw anywhere. Why, King Ethbaal himself would be proud to have a piece like this on his table."

Danel nodded, his eyes round.

Adaliah took a large bowl from a shelf and removed the oiled cloth covering a lump of creamy goat cheese. This bowl was another of Itthobaal's pieces, and a fine one. The glaze with which it had been finished matched that of the water jar she'd filled, a crystalline sea-green with the faintest hint of copper, a blend of Itthobaal's making. The words of the women came back to her. Though he would be quick to turn a profit given the chance, no one could doubt that Itthobaal's pottery was among the most beautiful produced by anyone in Zarephath.

"Will you show me how to make a cup like yours, Abba?"

The admiration in the child's tone brought a smile to her face. Danel looked up to his father, and the realization never failed to soothe even the foulest of Itthobaal's moods.

Adaliah set the platter containing their meal on the mat and sank onto her own cushion.

"What is this?" Itthobaal picked up an olive and held it between his thumb and forefinger. "I'm sick to death of olives. Where are the dates?"

"There were none in the market." She worked hard to keep her tone even. "Nor grapes either. The drought has frightened people. Instead of selling what they have, they hold it close."

Disgusted, he tossed the olive back onto the platter and snatched up a cake of barley bread. He smeared on a thick layer of cheese. "When Maresheh set a meal before me there were always dates." He lifted the bread and cheese to his mouth and paused to eye her over it. "She knew my likes. After nearly five years, I'd think you would have learned."

Adaliah lowered her gaze and bit her tongue. Had she not just told him there were no dates to be found in all of Zarephath? She picked up an olive and bit into it. They may not be Itthobaal's favorite, but they grew in abundance in the area around Zarephath. She'd become adept at curing and seasoning them, and she relished the salty, slightly bitter taste that invaded her mouth. Next time a bit more coriander, if she could find some.

Across the mat, Itthobaal munched his bread and focused his attention on Danel. "Yes, I will certainly teach you to make cups, and pots and bowls and jars as well. One day you will run my kiln."

"I will?" The boy's eyes grew round. "When?"

Itthobaal chuckled at the eager question. "When I'm too old to kick the wheel."

At the unexpected show of mirth, Adaliah dared to lift her eyes. The pride on his face as he gazed at his son stirred her heart. Danel could always make his father smile like none other. Her gaze strayed to a crumb nestled in his beard, which was more gray than black these days. His hair too was heavy with silver. When he had first come to Sidon to claim her as his bride, her spirits had fallen when she saw that her new husband's hair had more gray than her own father's had. She'd hoped to marry a younger man, someone kind and handsome, for whom she could make a happy home. Within hours, that hope lay dead on the floor of her bridal chamber.

Yet the union had brought her the most prized blessing of all.

Danel picked up his own cup and gazed at it, dark eyes full of wonder. "One day I will make even better cups than this."

Her breath caught in her chest. Would Itthobaal take the childish comment as an implied insult? Had she voiced it he surely would have.

But he threw back his head and laughed, clearly delighted with the boy's enthusiasm. "To be sure. But not for a long time, my eager son. You have much to learn." He popped an olive into his mouth. "Would you like to begin today?"

Danel's face lit. "I may go with you to the kiln today?"

"Yes. It is time you learn the trade."

The child's delighted gaze flew to Adaliah. "Will Imma come too?"

The question elicited a scornful blast. "To my kiln?"

Danel looked at her, concerned. "But you will be alone all day."

She had no chance to reply.

"She will stay here and try to make a decent evening meal for our return." Itthobaal's tone underwent a change when directed toward her. "I expect something other than olives. And at least an attempt at good bread." He tossed a crust on the platter. "I almost cracked a tooth biting into an unground kernel. After nearly five years I would think you could manage a better cake of bread."

Though the rebuke stung, such a look of worry covered Danel's face that she pasted on a smile. "I have plenty of work to fill my time," she told him. "And I'll visit the market to see if any of the sellers will part with a few dates." Her smile deepened. "Or perhaps an apple."

The mention of his favorite fruit brightened the boy's expression. She left the platter on the mat and tied Danel's sandals. He had yet to master tying, his small fingers awkward with the thin leather strips. He watched the procedure intently, always eager to learn. In that way he was more like her than his father, who bristled at any change to his everyday routine. She kept her movements slow so he could see. Then she helped him don his outer tunic.

When she straightened, Itthobaal grabbed her upper arm in a fierce grip and jerked her face close to his, his eyes glittering.

"I give you coin to buy food, since you can't seem to grow any on your own." His breath stank of last night's wine. "If I see no better return for my money than that"—he jerked his chin toward the dining mat—"maybe I will pay Tanytha to cook my meals."

He released her with a shove that sent her stumbling backward as he stomped out the doorway. The threat of inviting his daughter, whom he clearly considered as capable as her late mother, sent a cold shiver down Adaliah's spine. Tanytha would love nothing better than to announce Adaliah's ineptitude to the entire village.

Danel came close and tilted his head to look up at her. He gestured for her to bend close to him and when she did, he whispered, "I like olives."

Then they were gone. She stared after them, rubbing her arm, where a bruise would surely appear by evening.

Adaliah dribbled a bit of water over a wilting potato plant. The time to harvest lay weeks away still, but from the looks of the pitiful plant the yield would be meager. In years past her small courtyard garden had produced a generous array of potatoes, carrots, cucumbers, and celery that had made her chest swell with pride, even though Itthobaal insisted that Maresheh's garden had always proven more bountiful. Now the sandy soil was dry and cracked, without enough moisture to properly nourish even an onion.

The priests who served at the gods' temple placed the blame for this drought on a Hebrew prophet who commanded the skies to subdue the rain and the ground to hold back the dew. His reason, they said, was to force King Ahab to put aside his wife, Jezebel, because she lived a life completely devoted to Baal. They pronounced elaborate curses on all prophets of the Hebrew God and claimed victory when they announced that the queen's guards had unearthed yet another hiding place and put the false prophets to the sword. And yet the drought continued.

Adaliah let a few more drops of water fall from her jug onto a sadly drooping carrot plant. Sightings of the princess—now Ahab's queen—had been a regular occurrence during her childhood. Princess Jezebel had enjoyed frequent excursions into various parts of Sidon, always accompanied by a full complement of palace soldiers. When the trumpeters announced the advancing royal party, Adaliah and her friends would race to the roof of whatever house was closest, eager for an unimpeded view of the beautiful princess. For the next several days their conversations focused on the princess's shining raven hair, her silken gowns, the gemstones set in gold that adorned her fingers, wrists, and neck.

A loud bleating drew Adaliah's attention to the small olive tree, where their goat Boz was tied. She straightened, massaging an ache from the small of her back, careful not to spill a drop of the precious water. Boz bleated again, the sound reminiscent of Danel's cries when he was an infant.

"You wouldn't have to be tied up if you could be trusted not to eat the vegetables," she told the unhappy animal.

As if the drought wasn't devastating enough on her garden, Boz's taste for vegetables had destroyed her cucumbers when he escaped his pen a few weeks ago. Itthobaal had come home to find Adaliah weeping and a fretful Danel trying to comfort her. He became so enraged he aimed a series of kicks at the poor animal, until Danel threw his spindly arms around Boz's neck to protect her. Instead Itthobaal loosed his wrath on the small pen, which still lay in a pile of splinters. Then he pointed an accusing finger at Adaliah for her inability to manage her household as a good wife should.

She shuddered at the memory. That had not been a good night.

"I know you're hungry, but we need these potatoes," she told the goat.

She covered the distance between them and poured water into the urn she kept beneath the tree for Boz. The goat drank it dry and then looked up, her expression hopeful. Adaliah placed a hand on the animal's head and scratched the coarse hair between the horns. Boz had grown thinner in recent weeks and her milk less plentiful, ever since the shepherd charged with taking a small flock into the plains had declared that steps must be taken to ration the dwindling grasses there. The village leaders had responded by limiting the flock's grazing to half days in an effort to prolong the inevitable.

"I'll go to the cistern tonight," she promised Boz.

Water collected in the giant pit was deemed useful for animals, on which the clear well water should not be wasted. Zarephath's cisterns were being emptied at an alarming rate, and no new rain had fallen to refill them. Before long, there would be no water for the animals at all, and then…

She turned her head to look toward the house, where the statue of Baal stood near the doorway leading into the main floor of the house. When she arrived in Zarephath as a bride, Itthobaal told her it had been crafted by his father's own hands and baked in the kiln that had provided his family's livelihood since his grandfather's day. Privately she thought it a grotesque depiction of the god, with horns protruding from its head and its arms thrown wide. In one hand it held a thunderbolt in the shape of a spearhead. The expression on its bull-shaped face was one of cruelty, and it never failed to send a shiver down Adaliah's spine. She much preferred the statue she'd brought from her father's home in Sidon, which stood on a shelf in their bedchamber. That image of the god's face had no features, and its body was formed of graceful curves as suited the god of fertility.

Of course, Baal was also the god of storms and rain, was he not? She lifted her gaze to where the afternoon sun glittered in a clear blue sky. He wasn't attending to his chores lately. Or maybe the God that Hebrew prophet served had bested the mighty Baal in the matter of rain and dew.

Shocked by the irreverent thought, she gave Boz's head a final rub and hurried toward the house. When she passed the god's image, she averted her eyes lest he see the blasphemous thoughts in them.

She entered the living chamber to find Tanytha standing at her worktable, peeking beneath the oiled cloth that covered the remains of the goat cheese. The woman snatched her hand back, guilt flashing onto her face. A moment later the expression disappeared, replaced with one of haughty arrogance that reminded Adaliah sharply of her father.

"Tending to that pitiful patch of garden, were you?" Even the woman's voice held the same snide tone as Itthobaal's.

In the past five years Adaliah had become adept at hiding her emotions behind a cool mask of pleasant indifference. "The past months have not been kind to my garden," she admitted. "Though I'm sure your harvest will be as plentiful as your mother's always was."

Tanytha's eyes narrowed as though trying to decide whether to take the comment as a compliment or an insult. Apparently, she settled on the former. "Baal has gifted me with my mother's way with plants."

Adaliah bit back a comment to the effect that the god had better begin spreading that gift around, else he would have no worshippers left. Instead she carried the empty water jug across the room and set it beside the door, ready to be filled this evening when the sun's fierce rays were hidden behind the Great Sea.

"Abba and the boy paid me a visit on their way to the shop."

Tanytha's refusal to refer to Danel by name always set Adaliah's teeth on edge. The woman had hated Adaliah even before her arrival in Zarephath, and that feeling only intensified when Adaliah confided her pregnancy a short time later. At first Adaliah made excuses for Tanytha's intense dislike of her. How difficult it must be to welcome a stepmother into the home when her dear mother had been gone for only a few months. And with Danel's birth, how humiliating to see the father she adored transfer his affections from his only daughter to his newborn son.

Adaliah had cherished hopes that the enmity between them might pass when Tanytha wed Resheph, the handsome son of a maker of purple dye. But as the months, and then years, passed without a child of her own, Tanytha's dislike had deepened. Now, four years after her wedding night, the woman's waist was still as slim as a maiden's. She was barely civil to Danel, and only rarely to Adaliah.

"Did they?" Adaliah forced an agreeable expression. "That must have been pleasant."

Tanytha snorted. "Abba asked me if it was true that there were no dates to be found in the marketplace." She half turned toward the worktable and picked up a wrapped bundle Adaliah hadn't noticed before. "I told him I had no trouble finding dates and offered to bring some for his evening meal."

Now Adaliah did have trouble suppressing a grimace. When Itthobaal returned he would accuse her of lying.

"How kind of you," she managed to say. "From whom did you buy them? I've asked everywhere in the market."

"What do you expect? You're an outsider in Zarephath." Tanytha straightened her shoulders. "I'm one of them, something you will never be."

The statement slapped Adaliah. It was true. She didn't have a single friend in the entire village, thanks, she suspected, to the vicious tongue of the woman standing in front of her. The memory of Maresheh cast a deep, dark shadow in which Adaliah was completely hidden from view. She was an outsider in the village, just as she was an outsider in her own home.

She drew a slow breath into her chest and let it out silently before she dared speak. "Thank you for your gift for our table."

Tanytha's mouth hardened into a brittle line. "The gift is for Abba and no one else. Don't think for a minute that I won't know if he is robbed of a single date."

She slammed the bundle back on the worktable and stormed out of the house.

In the silence that followed, Adaliah stared at nothing and battled fearsome thoughts. Without a doubt, Itthobaal would point out Tanytha's success in procuring his favorite fruit, with an emphasis on Adaliah's failure. What he might say didn't worry her.

But oh! How she feared what he might do.

# CHAPTER TWO

Adaliah's nerves refused to settle in the hours after Tanytha's departure. When the day's bread was ready for the evening meal—with special attention paid to grinding the grain until the flour was fine enough to serve at King Ethbaal's palace in Sidon—she tidied every item in the small house, both downstairs in the main living areas and the bedchamber she shared with Itthobaal, and upstairs in Danel's small room and the others they used for storage. She beat the ever-present dust out of the sleeping mats. She trimmed the wicks on the lamps. She even replenished the wood for the cooking pit from the pile outside, though that was Danel's chore. At length she could find nothing else to do, no task to busy her hands and her mind.

An apple. She had promised Danel the treat for the evening meal. Relieved to have an errand to distract her thoughts, she took her scarf from its peg and arranged it over her head and wound it around her neck. Then she picked up her market basket and left the house.

The sun had started its descent, though it still rode high enough in the sky that she judged she had several hours before Itthobaal and Danel returned from the kiln. She patted the pouch hanging from her belt, which held her allowance of coins. Maybe a fish on the supper tray this evening would please Itthobaal enough that he would not mention her failure in the matter of the dates. Several stalls in the marketplace offered fish, but she decided on a different course. The short walk to the harbor would be pleasant, and the sea breeze cooling. She had plenty of time to get there, purchase a fish, and stop at the market for an apple or two on the way home.

When she left the last building behind, Adaliah paused to inhale a deep salty breath. She scanned her surroundings. Zarephath lay atop a ridge, bordered on one side by the Great Sea and on the other by the wide plain in which the villagers' livestock grazed. Two promontories extended into the sea, and from this vantage point she could see the smaller northern harbor. Thick groves of olive trees lay all around. The bitter fruit grew in abundance in the arid climate and sandy soil and provided a major portion of the village's livelihood. Exports of olives, and especially of olive oil, were second only to the fine pottery for which Zarephath was best known.

Her gaze strayed to the columns of smoke rising into the sky from the village. No less than twenty kilns contributed to the village's thriving pottery industry, the best of all owned by Itthobaal. The northernmost kiln was his, and she looked in that direction. No smoke rose from the squat stone building at the moment. They must be throwing pots today, readying them for firing tomorrow. Itthobaal would be showing his son how to kick the wheel, how to work the clay until it became pliable in his small hands. A proud smile tugged at the corners of her lips. One day that shop would be Danel's. She had no doubt at all that her son would produce even finer pots than his father.

Putting Zarephath to her back, she began the steep descent to the harbor. The trail was narrow but well worn. She walked quickly, shielding her eyes with one hand from the dazzle of the sunlight dancing on the ocean's surface. White-capped waves moved in their eternal rhythm, rushing toward the shore to deposit foam along the sandy beach before returning to the depths. The sight could be both mesmerizing and calming. Oftentimes she brought Danel here to watch as she told him how Baal became king of the gods in a fierce battle with Yamm, the god of the seas. He loved hearing the stories and devoured them with an eagerness that thrilled her. Danel's thirst for knowledge would grow as he did, until one day maybe he would learn so much he might even serve as advisor to the king of Sidon. Or advisor to the Hebrew King Ahab and his queen, Jezebel.

Adaliah halted her rambling thoughts with a laugh. All mothers held high hopes for their children. But her lofty goals for her son were mere fancy. Besides, a life lived among kings could certainly not be described as peaceful, since they were always at odds with one another. No, better the simple life of a potter for Danel, with a beautiful wife who gave him sons of his own and made him a happy home.

Her foot stumbled on the last thought as she neared the bottom of the path. Before she could stop herself, she tumbled to the ground. The basket flew out of her grip as she braced herself for the fall, and she landed hard on her hands and knees. Tears of pain blurred her vision.

A crash sounded nearby, and then footsteps approaching at a run pounded in her ears.

"Are you hurt?" a man's voice asked.

"I—" She sank back into a crouch and rubbed her stinging palms. "I don't think so."

"Here. Let me help you up."

A hand slipped beneath her arm, and she found herself being raised to her feet. The man squeezed the bruise left by Itthobaal that morning, and a new pain stabbed her. She sucked in a hissing breath.

The grip was immediately removed. "*Slicha.* I didn't mean to hurt you."

"No," she hurried to say, blinking away tears. "You didn't. I'm just…" She managed a laugh. "I'm embarrassed at being so clumsy."

The man standing before her was tall enough that she had to tilt her head to look at him. Dark hair, black as midnight, gleamed in the afternoon light. He looked to be a few years her senior, with a short beard and generous lips, and the unmistakable hooked nose of a Hebrew man. It struck her then that he'd said *I'm sorry* in Hebrew. Not unusual in this region of Sidon, but she hadn't heard the language since her grandmother spoke it when Adaliah was a child.

She tore her gaze from his face and glanced around. Her basket had tumbled down the remainder of the path.

"I'll get that for you." Moving with the grace of one accustomed to physical labor, he retrieved the object and returned it to her.

She thanked him in Hebrew. *"Todah."*

A smile lit his face. "You are Hebrew?"

"No, but my grandmother was."

"Ah." He nodded toward her hands. "Are you hurt?"

"I'm fine."

She kept her eyes averted, fixed on the ground beside him, aware that not far away the harbor buzzed with activity. If she were seen speaking alone with a man, and if that were to get back to Itthobaal…

She clutched her basket close to her body. "Thank you again."

A grin took his lips, and he responded in Hebrew. *"Al lo davar.* I'll get back to work then."

While she remained where she was, he gathered up a pile of long wooden strips that lay in a heap on the ground. He must have been carrying them and thrown them down when he saw her fall. Hefting the burden onto one shoulder, he nodded a final farewell and paced in the direction of the northern harbor.

Her hands and knees stinging, Adaliah continued on her errand.

Fortune was with her, and she arrived at the wooden pier to find a fishing boat had just returned with a full load. The crew stood at waist-high shelves gutting their catch to prepare them for the short journey to the village marketplace. She purchased a medium-size fish, plenty big enough to feed three, and watched as the sailor beheaded, gutted, and scraped the scales from its slimy body. Then, with the fish stored in her basket, she began the steep uphill climb toward the village.

By the time she reached the top of the ridge her breath came in heaves, and her scarf was damp with perspiration. Salty beads dripped down her forehead and into her eyes, the sting causing a flood of tears. She stopped to catch her breath and wipe her eyes with the tail of the scarf.

When she looked up, her gaze strayed to the northern edge of the village where Itthobaal's shop and kiln lay. A ribbon of smoke rose into the sky. Odd, since the kiln had been unlit not long ago. Why would he begin the lengthy firing process this late in the day? As she watched, the ribbon billowed and black smoke belched upward. Fingers of alarm pricked the back of her neck, sending a wave of gooseflesh down her arms. That smoke did not look like it came from the steady, even fire of a kiln.

She broke into a run, eschewing the path to cut across the ridge's uneven ground in the most direct route. Panic clutched at her chest as her feet pounded the dried grass. Her life, her heart, was in that shop, working alongside his father. If anything happened to him, she wouldn't be able to live.

When she arrived, smoke streamed through the open shop windows. Beyond the shop, off to one side, the kiln stood dormant. As she'd feared. Without pausing, she burst through the doorway and then skidded to a halt. An acrid fog filled the building, burning her nostrils and clogging her lungs. Heat slammed into her, so intense she could only blink. At the back end of the shop blazed a wall of flames. Her eyes burned so that she had to force them not to stay shut.

"Danel!" She shrieked his name, her voice high pitched with fear.

"Imma."

She nearly wept at the sound of the beloved voice, barely heard above the roar of the fire. Acting more on instinct than on thought, she plunged through the smoke.

Toward the rear of the shop she found Danel huddled on the floor. She scooped him into her arms and whirled.

Behind her, a mighty cough sounded. "Adaliah."

Turning again, she blinked to see through the blackened air. There, on the floor, lay Itthobaal. She rushed forward, Danel clutched tight in her arms. Broken pottery crunched beneath her sandals, and she realized that the heavy mat covering the floor was littered with shards of hardened clay. A shelf lay across Itthobaal's body, trapping him beneath it. Blood seeped from a gash at his temple, dripping to pool beneath his head.

"Help me," he said, and then was wracked with another cough.

Roaring flames engulfed the entire rear of the shop, and the fiery wall sent out a heat so intense she couldn't breathe. The fire was spreading toward them, licking at a patch of dirt that wasn't covered by the floor mat. How could dirt burn? The answer came in an instant, when she smelled the pungent odor of lamp oil blended with the smoke.

"Can't…move." Itthobaal gave a feeble attempt to shove the heavy shelf off his body and then gave in to another wracking fit.

Throwing Danel across one shoulder—Why had he stopped crying? Why wasn't he moving?—she stooped and grabbed the wood. With all her might she heaved and managed to lift it a handsbreadth. But it was too heavy, and it fell from her grip. Itthobaal let out a scream as the weight slammed against his chest.

She needed something to use as a wedge. Glancing around, she saw nothing. The flames crackled, and another wave of smoke surged toward her. On her shoulder, Danel tensed and gave a weak cough. She had to get him out of here. Whirling, she dashed through the black haze toward the doorway.

The relief was immediate. Her lungs gulped in fresh air as she ran a short but safe distance from the burning shop. She stopped on the opposite side of the stone kiln and dropped to her knees. She laid Danel gently on the ground then hovered over him. His chest heaved with the effort to breathe, but a hacking cough hampered him.

"Danel." A sob squeezed her throat and choked the word.

"Adaliah!" Her name carried to her on a choking gasp from inside the shop.

She looked in that direction. Itthobaal still lay trapped inside. There must be something she could use to wedge the shelf off of him. But what?

Danel wheezed. Soot smudged the smooth skin of his cheeks. He rolled onto his side toward her, drew his knees up to his chest, and gasped, "Imma."

"It's all right." She laid a calming hand on her son's head. "You're safe."

She rubbed his back, willing air into his laboring lungs. "Breathe slowly, Danel."

Again Itthobaal's scream reached her, this time suffused with rage. "Where are you, you worthless wretch? Help me."

After giving Danel's back a final rub, she climbed to her feet. A quick scan of the area revealed nothing of use. She couldn't lift that heavy object without help.

Wait. The kiln burned wood from olive trees. This she knew from early in her marriage when Itthobaal had described his family business. Olive wood was dense, and therefore burned steadily. She looked around. Where did he keep the fuel for the kiln?

With a worried look at her son, she started toward the back of the kiln. Maybe the wood was stored there.

She hadn't taken three steps when an explosion ripped through the air. A wave of heat so intense it felt like a physical blow nearly knocked her off her feet. She stopped and whirled toward the shop—in time to see the roof collapse inward.

# CHAPTER THREE

Adaliah stood rooted to the ground, staring in horror at the burning shop, when villagers began to arrive. A stream of running men rounded the side of the building.

The man in the lead, who looked vaguely familiar if only her numb brain would focus, caught sight of her. "Where is Itthobaal?" he shouted.

Dazed, she raised a hand and pointed toward the inferno.

A stunned silence descended. Every head turned in that direction, watching as flames from the roofless interior licked high into the sky. The walls, which were made of dressed stone, kept the fire contained, but as they watched, tongues of fire licked at the wooden front door.

"Get water," someone shouted.

Two men ran in the direction of the cistern, even as more people arrived. The crowd swelled, and people jostled to get to the front for a better view.

"Stop," the first man shouted after the two would-be rescuers, his voice full of authority. "We can't afford to waste it." He glanced at Adaliah, his expression apologetic. "Water will do him no good now."

She recognized him now. Fayez. He was the chief priest in Baal's temple, and therefore an acknowledged leader in

Zarephath. She shut her eyes as the truth of his words struck her. Itthobaal was gone. Dead. Burned alive, while trapped beneath the heavy shelf she couldn't move.

Behind her, Danel moaned. Adaliah whirled to find him sitting up, his gaze fixed on the fiery building. She raced to his side as a coughing fit wracked his small body. She collapsed onto the dirt beside him then pulled him onto her lap and rocked him back and forth, crooning wordless comfort in his ears.

A shriek sounded from amid the crowd of onlookers. She looked up to see Tanytha shove her way to the front of the group. Without pausing, the woman threw herself toward the blazing shop. Two men dashed forward, grabbed her arms, and dragged her back.

"My abba," she wailed, struggling to free herself. "Help him!"

The men held tight, and after a moment she sagged between them, held upright only by their grip on her arms. She raised her head and gave voice to her grief with a guttural keening that sliced through even the roar of the flames. Other women in the crowd took up the cry, and the sound of mourning rose into the heavens.

Danel's breath was coming more easily, and the horrible hacking had ceased. He stirred in her arms, trying to turn around toward the source of the weeping. Adaliah pulled him close, rocking him as she did when he was a babe.

"Let me through!"

A newcomer thrust through the onlookers. Resheph, Tanytha's husband. He cast one horrified glance toward the building and then gathered his grieving wife in his arms.

Suddenly, Tanytha's wailing fell silent. She stiffened and whirled.

"You!" Her eyes wild, she pointed a finger at Adaliah. "You did this. You killed him."

"Tanytha, shhh." Resheph held her in place with a firm grip on her shoulders.

"Look at her," Tanytha shrieked. "She was inside. There's soot all over her."

Adaliah shrank beneath the weight of the people's stares.

"I—" Her arms tightened around Danel. "I had to get my son out. The fire was spreading so quickly."

Fayez took a step toward her, his expression stony. "You were in the shop when the fire started?"

Adaliah shook her head. "I saw the smoke and ran inside. My son was in there."

"No one cares about your son." Tanytha's screech sliced into Adaliah's ears, and she winced. "What about my abba?"

"He—he was trapped," she stammered.

"You saw Itthobaal inside?" Fayez asked.

She nodded. The image was seared into her mind's eye. "A shelf fell on him. Danel was trying to pull him out. But the smoke was so thick. I had to get Danel to safety."

Tanytha let out a shriek. "You saved that worthless boy and left my abba to die?"

The words flew like darts and lodged in Adaliah's soul. Yes, that was what she had done. But she had to save her son, didn't she? The gods surely understood that.

"I tried to free him." She held Fayez's gaze, imploring him to believe her. "The shelf was too heavy."

"She lies!" Tanytha writhed against her husband's grip. "Abba took good care of her, but she resented him. She's a terrible wife, he told me so just this morning. She hated him and wished him dead."

"No!"

The protest flew from Adaliah's lips. But an instant later she flinched. Itthobaal had gone to visit his daughter this morning. To complain about her? And Danel had been there, hearing his father talk about what a bad wife she was. She shook her head in an effort to clear her thoughts. Did she hate Itthobaal?

Tanytha jerked out of Resheph's grasp and launched herself at Adaliah. Danel cried out and shrank deeper into her embrace. Moving quickly, Adaliah twisted away from her, so her body acted as a shield for Danel while Tanytha's fists beat her head, her back.

The blows stopped, and she opened her eyes to see Resheph drag his sobbing wife away. The crowd parted and the two disappeared, though the sounds of her grief still rang throughout the village.

Fayez came forward and knelt beside them. He touched Danel, whose face was pressed against Adaliah's chest, wetting her tunic with silent tears.

"Danel, you must talk to me." The priest spoke in a soft but insistent tone.

Slowly, Danel lifted his head. Tears continued to stream down his cheeks, but he gave Fayez his full attention.

"Did you see who started the fire?"

Adaliah sucked in a breath. Surely Fayez didn't believe the accusations of a hysterical woman. She looked up to find hostile expressions on many of the faces turned her way. Her stomach tightened into knots.

Danel shook his head.

Fayez extended a hand, and after a moment's hesitation, Danel took it. The priest pulled him from Adaliah's arms into a standing position. He held the child's hand sandwiched between his. Dozens of scars, both old and new, crisscrossed the man's arms and hands, evidence of the rituals he observed in worshipping Baal. At the sight of her son's small hand trapped between the priest's, Adaliah was taken by a chill that came from a fearful place deep inside. She'd watched Fayez wield the sacrificial knife in countless temple rituals, watched him spill the blood of worshippers to please the god. She wanted to snatch Danel out of his reach. Instead she wrapped her arms around her middle, hugged herself, and bit her tongue.

"Tell me what happened," Fayez said.

"Abba showed me how to work the clay," the child answered. "It wouldn't do what I wanted, but I tried. I tried and tried."

Fayez nodded encouragement, his gaze locked onto the boy's face.

"Then I was sleepy, and Abba said I could lay down for a while. He made a pallet in the little room where he keeps the clay and the colors. And then I heard a loud sound. Like a crash."

The shelf falling? She remembered the smashed pottery littering the floor. Such a heavy shelf could not have fallen on its own. Had Itthobaal somehow pulled it over on himself?

"I came out, and Abba wouldn't answer me. He just lay there."

The flow of his tears increased, and his little chest heaved with suppressed sobs. Adaliah squeezed her hands into fists to keep from pulling him into the comfort of her arms.

"He was lying on the ground?" Fayez asked.

Danel nodded. "Like Imma told you. The shelf fell on him, and all his pots broke. I tried to get it off, but I couldn't move it. And then there was a fire, and it was scary." He was weeping freely now, the words coming in gulps.

Fayez gave the small hand a jerk. "How did the fire start?"

But Danel could only shake his head, unable to stop the shuddering sobs.

"Lamp oil." The words left Adaliah's tongue before she could stop them. Fayez turned a sharp look on her. "I—I remember smelling lamp oil when I was trying to lift the shelf off of Itthobaal. He may have been trying to get something from the top of the shelf, and pulled it over, and the lamp broke and the oil caught." She was babbling now, voicing thoughts as they came to her. She shut her mouth.

The priest's eyes narrowed, and she had to struggle not to look away from the piercing gaze. After a moment he tilted his face toward the sky and spread his arms wide.

"Why would Itthobaal light a lamp in full daylight?"

An unspoken accusation lurked behind the question. Part of her quaked at the veiled blame, while the other felt nothing but relief that he had released Danel's hand.

"The shop has windows on only one side." She wet her lips, grasping for an acceptable explanation. "He may have been etching a design into a piece and needed the extra light."

A murmur rose from the watchers, a combined tone of disbelief. A quick glance in that direction showed her that many of them were watching the inquisition with eager expressions, waiting for the priest to pronounce his verdict.

She turned her attention back to Fayez. "I don't know why. I wasn't there. But I did smell lamp oil."

A shout came from the crowd. "Where were you, then?"

Adaliah did not look away from Fayez. "I was in the harbor buying a fish for our evening meal."

"Where's the fish?"

Adaliah recognized the voice as belonging to Keprea, one of Tanytha's friends. She glanced around the area for her basket. There was no sign of it.

"I—I must have dropped it when I saw the smoke."

Keprea's reply dripped scorn. "You paid good money for a fish and then threw it away?"

Fayez's eyes narrowed again, and his stare was so intense Adaliah fought an urge to scurry from his sight.

She swallowed against a desert-dry throat. "Send a man to the harbor to ask the fishermen. He will doubtless find my market basket along the way." Switching her gaze to Keprea, she added, "With the fish still inside."

After another long moment, Fayez jerked a nod. "It will be as you say."

He rose and extended a hand downward to help Adaliah stand. She hesitated only a moment and managed not to shiver when her fingers touched his. Once on her feet, Danel wrapped his arms around her legs and buried his face in her tunic.

Resting a protective hand on the child's back, she said, "I must get my son home. He has endured much this day." She lifted her chin and spoke in a voice loud enough to carry to the back of the crowd. "As have I."

Let that serve as a reminder that she too had suffered a loss.

Her shoulders stiff, she guided Danel toward home. The onlookers parted to allow them passage. She felt the burden of their accusing eyes with every step but kept her head high and her face an impassive mask.

She dared not let them glimpse the guilty thought that pulsed through her mind. No longer would she be subjected to Itthobaal's vicious tongue and harsh treatment. She was free of him.

And she was glad.

# CHAPTER FOUR

"D o we have enough now, Imma?" Danel kicked at the mound of halfa grass with a sandaled toe.

Adaliah inspected their harvest. The grasses were drier than she liked and would probably crumble when she wove them into coils to make a new market basket. But at least the morning's errand had served its primary purpose, to distract Danel from his grief over the distressing loss of his abba. The child had woken screaming multiple times in the two nights since the fire, and she had moved him from his bedchamber upstairs down to hers.

"I think so." She knelt and tied the cords around the grass to form a bale.

In truth they had barely enough to make a good start. The grasses all around them had been picked nearly clean by Zarephath's herds, and the few scraggly patches left were quickly becoming brittle from lack of dew or rain.

"I can carry it," he said when the task was done.

He easily picked up the bundle, yet more proof that the harvest wouldn't prove worthwhile for basket weaving. But at least they could feed the grasses to Boz.

They set off across the plain, Adaliah setting a short stride so Danel could keep up without straining. The olive trees that dotted the landscape provided the only spots of color in the otherwise dreary vista. Dry, brittle grass covered the area in a buff-colored picture of desolation. Even the buildings of Zarephath appeared dull and drab. At the sight of smoke rising in columns from various kilns throughout the village, vivid images surfaced in her mind. The fiery wall sending a finger of flame across the dirt. Itthobaal struggling beneath the shelf, his cheek stained with blood. She shut her eyes but could not banish the memories. Or the searing guilt that accompanied them.

*"Where are you, you worthless wretch? Help me!"*

Would that voice echo in her head forever?

They arrived at the southern edge of the village. When Danel made for the central road, Adaliah stopped him.

"Let's go this way." She pointed toward a path that lay along the westernmost buildings. "That way we can feel the wind from the sea."

In truth she wanted to save the child from the suspicious stares and whispers she had encountered with every trip to the well or the cistern in the past three days. No one had spoken directly to her since the fire, but they made sure to speak to one another loudly enough for her to overhear.

"…not a good wife…"

"She left her husband…"

"I heard she…"

The child complied without question, and they arrived at their home with no unpleasant encounters.

Until they stepped inside.

Tanytha stood near the cook stone, her arms folded tightly over her chest. After one look at the savage expression on her face, Adaliah turned to Danel.

"Go and give Boz some water. The jar is outside, beside the door."

Danel hesitated, casting a cautious glance toward Tanytha. He had never been at ease around his half sister, no doubt sensing the contempt in which she held him. Then, with a nod, he deposited the bundle of grasses in the corner and disappeared through the courtyard door.

The moment the child was out of sight, Tanytha launched a verbal attack.

"You killed him," she spat. "I know you did."

The vicious accusation slapped Adaliah, who winced as though struck. "I know you're distraught—" she began.

"You know nothing of my feelings!" Tanytha's shout echoed from the stone walls. "I loved him, but you? You hated him."

A heated reply rose to Adaliah's lips, but she pressed them together and sealed it behind. This woman had lost her beloved father.

"Itthobaal was my husband." Mercifully, she was able to keep her tone calm. "I did not hate him."

A sudden shaft of shame sent heat into her cheeks. Did she hate Itthobaal? She certainly had reason enough.

"Your lies are etched on your face. They told me how they found you, standing there and watching the fire burn his shop. How you just stood there, doing nothing."

"I tried." She clasped her hands in front of her mouth, pleading for understanding. "The shelf was too heavy. I tried to move it, but I couldn't."

"Then you should have died at his side."

She squeezed her hands tighter. "I had to save Danel. I was looking for something to use as a wedge."

Tanytha continued as if she hadn't spoken. "You didn't even call for help. If you didn't strike the flint that started that fire, you caused it to happen." Her eyes narrowed to slits. "If you paid someone, I will find him."

The ridiculous accusation drew a bitter laugh from Adaliah. "Paid someone? With what? I'm barely given enough coin to buy food and necessities."

The woman's lip curled. "There are many ways a woman can pay a man."

The implication so disgusted Adaliah that her stomach churned. She pressed a fist into her middle. What kind of person would think such thoughts?

*One who is crazed with grief.*

She drew a calming breath. "You are distraught, and with good reason. But think of Danel. He, too, has lost his abba. And I have lost my husband." Gathering every ounce of compassion she could scrape together, she took a step forward, her hand extended. "We can be of comfort to one another."

Tanytha drew herself up, outrage apparent in her stiff posture. "What do I care for that plague of a child? He has been a curse on me from his first breath. I wish he had never drawn a second."

Adaliah dropped her arm and squeezed her hands into fists. The poison spewing from the woman before her nearly robbed her of breath. She found no words to reply.

"Why don't you take *your son* and go back to Sidon, where you belong? There's nothing here for you. No one wants you here."

Tension evaporated from Adaliah's clenched fingers. The suggestion, though cruelly intended, was worth considering. Tanytha was right about one thing. She had no friends in Zarephath. The only tie she and Danel had was her husband's daughter, who clearly wanted to be rid of them. Would Father let her return to his home? She knew he would. He would welcome the presence of his grandson and would train him in the ways of a weaver of fine rugs, alongside her older sister's sons.

But Danel would be the youngest by far. Though he would learn his grandfather's trade, the knowledge would be his only inheritance. Whereas if he stayed in Zarephath, he would one day have this house as his own, and Itthobaal's kiln as well. He would not learn the skills he needed from his father, but other skilled potters lived in Zarephath. Once the scandal of Itthobaal's death had receded to memory, surely one of them would be happy to take an intelligent, eager boy on as an apprentice.

She lifted her chin and met Tanytha's hard gaze. "We belong here." She spread her arms wide to indicate the room around them. "This is our home."

Fury blazed in her stepdaughter's eyes. "This house is rightfully mine. You and your son are intruders."

Rightfully hers? That couldn't be right. Tanytha might wish it, since she and Resheph lived in his father's house along with his brother and his brother's family. The claim was nothing more than a taunt.

Adaliah was spared from answering when Tanytha strode toward her. She thrust her face forward until barely a finger's breadth separated them.

"When I find proof that you killed my abba, I'll expose you for the murderer you are. And I will throw the first stone that speeds you to your death."

When she had gone, the strength leeched from Adaliah's body. She collapsed onto a cushion, her pulse throbbing wildly in her ears.

Tanytha's cruel words echoed in Adaliah's mind throughout the day. Did others in the village think her responsible for Itthobaal's death? She didn't mind being the subject of gossip, but if enough people believed the talk, her life could truly be in danger. If she were killed, what would happen to Danel?

Late in the afternoon, when most of the villagers would be resting during the heat of the day, she made her way to the temple. She had heard nothing from Fayez since the fire. Had he spoken with the fisherman from whom she'd bought her fish to support her claim of innocence? His word held weight with everyone in Zarephath.

The temple lay at the center of the village. Though this one was small compared to the temple in Sidon, it had been crafted with the care and attention due the gods. Columns lined the shaded portico, their ornate caps etched with gold. Lined atop the pitched roof was a row of carvings, depictions of the constellations from which the gods ruled. A set of wide steps led through an archway and into the inner court. Adaliah made her way up, aware that she drew stares from the few people who were out. Her skin itched beneath the weight of their gazes. She had never been truly accepted in Zarephath, but she'd usually been received cordially.

The coppery odor of fresh blood filled the inside courtyard of the temple. A few worshippers gathered around the shrines of Astarte and Melqart, though no ceremony was underway at the moment. More filled the inner sanctuary, the shrine of Baal. Priests, identifiable by their shaved faces and ankle-length crimson robes, worked at the far end of the paved court, near the ramp where the sacrificial animals were brought into the temple. Others worked at the altar, cleaning away the remains from the morning's rituals.

Adaliah approached the nearest priest. "I would like to speak to Fayez. Is he here?"

The man looked her up and down and then gave a nod. He held up a hand, indicating she should wait, and without speaking disappeared through the doorway leading to the priests' quarters. She had not waited long when Fayez appeared.

"The boy is well?" he asked. "No ill effects from the fire?"

Though the question was politely asked, his eyes remained hard.

"He is unhurt, but his dreams are tormented."

Fayez dipped his head in a nod. "That is to be expected. They will pass."

An unexpected fit of nerves took Adaliah, and she clasped her hands in front of her to keep them from trembling. "I had a visit from Tanytha this morning. She believes I caused the fire that killed her abba."

He cocked his head sideways, peering closely at her. "And did you?"

"No!" The word shot from her mouth like an arrow.

"Then you have no cause for concern."

"Tanytha has many friends," she said. "They will listen to her, and I fear for my son's safety if the gossip isn't put to rest quickly."

He dismissed the idea with a flip of his hand. "Itthobaal's death was an accident. His daughter is distraught. People will understand that."

"If you say it, they will."

His eyebrows rose. "You wish to involve the chief priest of Baal in the petty pursuits of blathering women?"

Heat rushed into Adaliah's cheeks. "I apologize. I'm only thinking of my son's welfare. Were you able to speak with the man from whom I bought the fish?"

"Yes," he said impatiently. His gaze strayed to the priests working at the altar. "And your basket was found on the ridge, just as you said."

She swallowed against a dry throat. "If you could tell—"

He cut her off. "I will verify the truth to anyone who asks." He started to turn away and then stopped. His expression became curious. "What will you do now?"

The question had hovered at the edge of her mind since the fire. In the near future she would need to find a way to support Danel and herself. She had a few skills, such as sewing and basket weaving.

"Will you stay here?" Fayez asked when she didn't reply. "As I recall your family is from Tyre."

"Sidon," she corrected. Tanytha's bitter words came back to her, that the house rightfully belonged to her. Were the laws of inheritance different in Zarephath than in Sidon? Since they were both under King Ethbaal's rule, they should be the same. "Itthobaal's house and kiln belong to me now, do they not?"

The priest nodded. "They're yours by widow's right." A humorless smile curved the edges of his lips. "If you decide to return to Sidon, you could offer them to the service of Baal. The god would certainly reward such a gift."

She answered in a determined tone that left no room for doubt. "We are staying here."

He dipped his head in acknowledgment and then turned away. Adaliah watched him disappear through the doorway to the priests' quarters before she left the temple. She would have liked to ask to have her basket back, but she hadn't the nerve to disturb the chief priest a second time.

The heat had begun to subside, so the trip home was pleasant. She reviewed the conversation as she walked. Widow's right, he said. She was a widow. The word felt odd when she applied it to herself.

But she would need to earn money, and soon. The few coins Itthobaal had given her for the market were nearly gone.

She came to an abrupt halt as a thought occurred to her. Itthobaal had always counted out her coins from the pouch he wore on his belt. A few more he stored in an earthen jar at home. The rest he kept in a cask at the shop. The cask had probably burned, but the coins would still be there.

She hurried home to get Danel.

"Here's a good one, Imma." Danel held up a bowl, charred but otherwise unharmed.

Upon their arrival at the pottery shop Adaliah had been surprised to discover that not everything inside was destroyed by the fire. Though nothing made of wood or cloth remained in any usable condition, some pieces of pottery had survived. She had sent Danel home to fetch a blanket they could use to bundle the pieces they salvaged. Tomorrow they would take them to the beach and wash the soot away with seawater. Perhaps she could sell them in the market.

"Put it with the others," she told him.

She combed through a pile of ash with a long stick, hoping for a glimpse of silver. Nothing.

Many of the items were still recognizable, like the scarred surface of a heavy worktable. The legs had been reduced to ash, but the thick wood slab had not burned all the way through. All that remained of the potter's wheel was the kick plate, and it had been splintered when the shelf fell on Itthobaal.

Nor was the heavy shelf burned completely. The men who had retrieved Itthobaal's remains had moved it to one side. Her stomach churned whenever she looked at the place where her husband died, where a man-sized section of the floor mat was not scorched. Upon entering the shop Danel had stood staring at that spot for a long time with tears sliding down his cheeks. Her heart ached for him, but she could find no words of comfort for such a loss.

The fire had not spread to the small side room where Itthobaal stored his dyes. A half-dozen vats stood there undisturbed, though she didn't know if the contents had been damaged by the heat. Perhaps one of the other potters in Zarephath would buy them.

Using her stick, she stirred a pile of shattered bowls but found no money beneath them.

"It isn't here, Imma."

She looked up to find Danel standing in the doorway, watching her with his hands on his hips, a stance Itthobaal had assumed often.

"It has to be." She was careful to filter the sense of hopelessness from her tone. "He kept it here somewhere."

"Maybe somebody took it."

The same idea had occurred to her. The men who carried Itthobaal's body away for the funeral rites, perhaps. They had certainly helped themselves to the pouch hanging from the dead man's corpse. Or anyone could have entered the shop once the fire burned itself out. The charred remains of the door had been standing open when they arrived.

Defeated, she dropped the stick. Why hadn't she remembered the cask sooner?

Danel picked his way through the debris and slipped his hand into hers. "Can we go home?"

Soot blackened the face he turned up to hers. Both their tunics were covered with ashes.

She squeezed his hand and managed a smile. "We'll stop at the cistern and fill one of these bowls so we can wash when we get home."

In the doorway she turned to scan the room one more time. She would have to come back and clear away the rubble. And eventually she would have to hire men to replace the roof, but that would wait. First, she needed to sell what remained of Itthobaal's goods. That would take care of them for a little while. In the meantime, she'd pray to the gods for a way to earn enough money to feed her son.

# CHAPTER FIVE

Adaliah propped the coiled basket—a different one, normally used at home for storage—on her hip as she walked. Beside her, Danel matched her pace, though he had to stretch his legs to do so.

"May we get more dates?" He turned an eager gaze up to her. "I like dates almost as much as apples."

She'd served the last of Tanytha's gift during their evening meal last night. It had taken her five days after the fire to work up the courage to eat them, certain that any moment the bereaved daughter would storm into her house and accuse her of killing Itthobaal just so she could feed the treat to her son.

After pulling Danel to a halt, she crouched before him and held his gaze. "If we see your sister in the market, make no mention of the dates."

Questions creased the smooth skin of his forehead. "Why?"

How could one explain unmerited hostility to a child?

"Because," she said, "Tanytha knows dates were your abba's favorite, and thinking of that will make her miss him even more."

Those liquid brown eyes softened with compassion. "Okay, Imma. We won't make Tanytha sad."

She pulled him into a quick hug. "Good boy."

The hum of voices from the market reached her as they rounded the last corner. Ahead, in the center of the square, lay the temple. In the open area before the ornate structure, merchants had set up stalls to display the wares they offered for sale. In times past the plaza was filled to overflowing, and the number of villagers who visited the stalls could not be easily tallied. Today she counted barely a dozen merchants and not many customers. The drought was striking at rich and poor alike.

The first few stalls offered items that held no interest for her, mostly fabric and housewares. She noted a variety of baskets, and a pinprick of concern stabbed at her. These baskets were finer than anything she could produce, even if she could harvest enough viable grasses. And there were no customers looking at this woman's baskets.

"Look, Imma." Danel ran up to a tented stall and picked up an item from the table. "It's a necklace of seashells."

He held the item out for her inspection. Dozens of tiny shells had been polished until they shone and strung together. In the center dangled a larger shell, its pink surface gleaming in the morning sunlight. The woman behind the table gave Danel an indulgent smile, no doubt hoping for a sale. When she raised her gaze and caught sight of Adaliah, the smile vanished.

"Put that down before you break it," she snapped.

The delight faded from his face. He returned the necklace to the table with extreme care and then turned a troubled look on Adaliah. The merchant, whose name she did not know, folded her arms across an ample bosom and fixed a stern stare on Adaliah.

Adaliah took Danel's hand. "Let's find an apple, shall we?"

She pulled the child away, but the incident burned like acid in her stomach. What had she done to alienate that woman? Was she a friend of Tanytha's?

Closer to the temple's colonnade stood the vegetable stands, though only a few were open today. She and Danel approached the first, which featured a sad assortment of shriveled cucumbers and a few wilted bundles of parsley.

She made a show of inspecting the display. "There aren't many people out this morning," she said.

The man seated behind the table answered with an affirmative grunt and did not rise from his stool. Adaliah picked up an undersized cucumber. The flesh felt soft between her fingers. Past its prime, but there wasn't much selection. She set the vegetable in her basket and shook out a coin from her pouch. As she placed the coin in the man's pudgy palm, a woman approached him at a run.

"What are you doing?" She snapped the question at the man, but her narrow-eyed glare settled on Adaliah.

Still seated on his stool, he scowled up at her. "What do you think?"

The woman waved a hand over the table and spoke this time to Adaliah. "My husband is addled in the brain. These aren't for sale."

Taken aback, Adaliah's mouth fell open.

"What do you mean, not for sale?" The man turned a disbelieving look on his wife. "Why am I sitting here if not to sell your pitiful vegetables?"

At a furious look from his wife, he fell silent. The woman took a cloth from beneath his stool and spread it over the table.

"We're closed," she told Adaliah.

Behind her, the man caught Adaliah's eye, clenched his fist around the coin, and jerked his head in a clear command. *Leave now.* Clutching her basket, and with Danel hovering close to her side, she moved away from the stall. As she left, the woman rounded on her husband and Adaliah heard a snatch of her hissing conversation.

"Don't you know who that is? We aren't—"

An invisible weight settled on her chest. With an effort she forced air into her lungs. As though sensing her discomfort, Danel slipped a hand into hers as they walked toward the next stall.

They were five steps away when the merchant, a woman Adaliah recognized from her morning trips to the well, unfolded a cloth and draped it over her table.

"I'm closed," she announced, and then turned her back.

Adaliah turned toward the next stall in time to see that merchant cover her bowls of apples and dates. Heart pounding against her ribcage, Adaliah stood still, watching as each of the half-dozen merchants offering vegetables or fish closed. Her head felt light, and she wavered on her feet.

Danel squeezed her hand. "I don't want an apple tonight, Imma."

The woman in the next stall twisted her lips into a smirk. "I hear the drought isn't so bad just north of here. They say there's food to be had in Sidon."

A sob stuck in Adaliah's throat. She couldn't think of a response and couldn't have voiced it if she had. Without a word, she and Danel left the marketplace.

"Why are all the people mad at us?" Danel asked that evening.

They were seated on their cushions, their evening meal on the mat between them. A sparse meal, to be sure. Olives, a small cake of bread for each of them, and a few thin slices of cucumber. Even so, Adaliah had to force herself to swallow each bite. Uncertainty churned in her stomach. Was Tanytha's plan to starve them out of the house she considered hers?

Her first impulse was to correct him with a platitude. *They don't hate us. We went to the market at the wrong time, that's all.* But she refused to lie to her son. *Because your sister hates us. Because she wants to drive us out of town so she can take what is rightfully yours. Because people are mean-spirited and merciless.* She struggled to come up with an answer that wouldn't frighten him.

"I don't know," she finally said.

He stared at her for a long moment, his expression unreadable. Then he nodded and bit into an olive.

A knock on the door rang in the room. Adaliah brushed the crumbs from her hands and got to her feet. *Don't let it be Tanytha with more of her taunts. Not in front of Danel.*

She opened the door to find not Tanytha, but a man.

Badahur owned several kilns in Zarephath and was rumored to be quite wealthy. Itthobaal had considered him a competitor, and though the two had been cordial in public, in private Itthobaal despised the man for engaging in what he claimed were dishonest dealings.

Though his lips curved into the semblance of a smile, he held her gaze with cold eyes. "May I come in?"

She stepped back and allowed him to enter. When he did, he halted in the center of the room, his gaze circling. A tall man with a muscular build, he seemed to shrink the room with his presence.

With a hand, he gestured toward the mat where Danel sat. "I apologize for disturbing your evening meal."

She shook her head to dismiss the apology.

"Is there a place we can talk privately?" His glance settled on the opening to the bedchamber.

Fire flamed in her face. "Danel, go out to the courtyard and take care of Boz. Feed him the last of the halfa grass."

The child looked from Badahur to her and then shoved the last bite of bread into his mouth. Scooping up an olive, he obeyed.

When they were alone, Adaliah eyed the man before her. Custom dictated that she offer a visitor to her home some gesture of hospitality, but she had little to give. Instead, she indicated a mat. "Would you like to sit?"

He declined with a shake of his head. "I won't be long. I've come with a business proposal. I would like to buy Itthobaal's kiln."

Though she managed to remain outwardly impassive, Adaliah's thoughts raced. This could be an answer to their predicament. The money from the sale would increase her meager stash of coins significantly. But if she sold the kiln, what would that leave Danel of his father's? And what would he do when he became a man? Young men who joined the family business were more assured of a secure future, something she wanted to provide for her son. Besides, Badahur owned several kilns already. What did he want with one more?

She tilted her head and studied him. "Why do you want another kiln?"

At first she thought he might not answer. He returned her stare, thoughts playing across his face.

Then his expression cleared. "Itthobaal's kiln is of a complex design. It employs a downdraft construction, whereas mine are crossdraft structures. And his has metal supports for the firebox, which are more expensive than clay but superior and longer lasting."

The explanation meant nothing to her besides the fact that Itthobaal's kiln was of a higher quality than the ones Badahur owned.

"But *my* kiln"—she emphasized the ownership and was satisfied to see his eyebrows rise—"is old. Built by my late husband's grandfather, according to him. Surely with the resources you possess you can build a newer and better one of your own."

A grudging smile curved the corners of his lips. He splayed his hands. "But why go to the trouble, when *yours* sits unused?"

A valid argument, but still Adaliah hesitated. Danel was too young to consult now, but would he one day resent her for selling the means of his family's livelihood, the occupation established two generations prior to his birth?

Badahur's fingers began a rhythmic tapping on his thighs. "What good is the kiln doing you? Sell it to me so it can continue to be used for the purpose for which it was built."

She decided to share her thoughts. "But then my son will have nothing of his father's family. What will he do when he is older? Itthobaal intended to train his son to work at his side and eventually take over the family business."

"Itthobaal's intentions died with him. There is no one to train the boy now."

An idea dawned on her. Itthobaal would have struck her for the suggestion, but he was no longer around. "You could train him."

Surprised, he slapped a hand to his chest. "Me?"

She nodded, the idea taking form in her mind. "You could take him on as your apprentice and teach him the ways of a potter. I would grant you free use of the kiln while he trains. Then when he is old enough to work on his own, he can take over the operation."

For a long moment he stared at her, his expression calculating. Hope blossomed in her chest.

A moment later it was crushed beneath the heel of Badahur's cruel laughter.

"I have six sons of my own, and that is too many apprentices. Why would I take on another? My offer is for your kiln, not for your son."

The scorn that fueled his laugh burned Adaliah like a flame. She stiffened. "Then my answer is no."

His gaze slid to the meal platter and then returned to her. "Reconsider. You would have plenty of money from the sale to care for your son and yourself for a long time to come."

Now it was her turn to give way to a bitter laugh. "What good will money do if no one will sell to me?"

The grim smile that appeared on his face told her he had heard about her experience that morning.

"I understand you encountered some difficulty in the marketplace. I can smooth things over with the merchants, given the right motivation." When she didn't answer, he took a step toward her. "Come now. Think about it. If you sell me your kiln, you and your son could remain here, in this house. I would let it be known you are under my protection." He extended a hand and ran a finger down her arm. "You're young still, and not unattractive."

The meaning of the gesture, and the lewd expression that settled on his face, sent a shiver through her body. She took an abrupt step backward.

"My answer is no," she repeated.

His gaze hardened, and his hand fell to his side. "So be it." With another glance at the platter, his lip curled. "Enjoy your evening meal."

When he had gone, Adaliah sank onto the cushion. A violent tremble ravaged her body, and it took her several minutes to stop the shaking.

# CHAPTER SIX

The ravine in which Elijah refuged reminded him of his home. Oftentimes he had retreated with his father's goats across the hilly terrain surrounding Tishbe, seeking the solitude and communion with Yahweh that nourished his soul more than any worldly food or drink ever could. Only here in Kerith there were no goats, nor much else but scrub bushes and the occasional thirsty olive tree.

He sat beneath one of those rain-starved trees, the scant shade providing shelter from the heat of the descending sun. A cramp in his calf reminded him that it had been hours since he began praying, and his legs needed to move. He stretched them out before him and leaned forward, sighing with relief as blood rushed to feed sore muscles.

"These bodies You created are frail vessels."

He aimed the comment at the sky, though he knew full well the Lord didn't need spoken words to hear him. Still sometimes, especially after hours of prayer, his ears craved the sound of a human voice. Even his own.

The divine response swelled in his spirit, a nearly tangible feeling of agreement tinged with humor.

Smiling, Elijah got to his feet and headed down the sloping hillside. At the bottom he knelt beside the brook that ran the length of the valley. The water had been reduced by more than half in the months since he arrived at this wadi. Soon it would slow to a trickle and then cease to run altogether.

He cupped his hands and scooped water. The moisture cooled his parched throat. Did the king of Israel yet feel the drought squeezing life from the land over which he ruled? For the sake of the people, Elijah prayed Ahab would come to his senses soon. However, that seemed unlikely as long as Jezebel had his ear.

Elijah splashed the back of his neck. That had been a match made by Satan and hatched in the depths of hades. Though the union with the daughter of Ethbaal of Sidon brought power and riches to Israel, the impact on the nation's people, and her king, had been devastating. Temples to Baal were being erected across the land. When would men learn that Yahweh's plans had nothing to do with worldly riches? And had the Lord not proven time and again that victory depended not on the strength of armies, but upon His will and His ways?

Elijah stood from the brook, noting again how its flow had diminished. Though he knew there was no need for concern—had Yahweh not proven a thousand times over that His hand would provide for Elijah's every need?—he lifted his gaze to the cloudless blue sky. "How long before I leave this place, Lord?"

*Soon. Soon.*

Two black specks appeared in the northern sky. He watched as they neared, until he could make out the strokes of their wings. A pair of ravens, each carrying a burden clutched in its claws. Bread and meat for his evening meal, further proof of the Lord's care.

Elijah sat down on the bank of the Brook Kerith and waited.

# CHAPTER SEVEN

"They are good bowls."

Adaliah thrust the ceramic piece at Hanibal's chest, perhaps a bit harder than necessary, but a growing feeling of desperation gave the gesture force. This was the third potter she had approached today with a simple request—take all Itthobaal's wares in exchange not for money but for food.

"They are," Hanibal agreed. "Itthobaal was renowned for his skill."

"A jar of grain is all I ask." She allowed a note of pleading to slip into her tone. If she had to beg to feed Danel, she would. "These are worth far more."

He stood in the shade of the canopy that covered the wide entry of his pottery workshop. Behind him his workers chatted over their labor, their voices blending with the whirring of several kick wheels. Through an open window Adaliah glimpsed a table covered with finished bowls, jars, and cups, none of them as fine in quality as the one in her hands.

"I have my own pieces to sell." He plucked a dirty cloth from his girdle and mopped sweat from his brow. "What would I do with his?"

*Use them as chamber pots for all I care.* She bit the comment back and replied instead, "Surely you can find some use for them. Or the money they would add to your purse if you sell them."

The arrogant way he looked down the length of his nose made her squirm with embarrassment. Gulping back her shame, she tried again.

"My husband considered you a friend. Will you not give one jar of grain to help his son?"

A smirk twisted his lips. "I hear there is plenty of grain in Sidon. Perhaps you should take him there."

She closed her eyes to hide from the disdain he projected. Tanytha had spread her poison widely. Every potter Adaliah had approached had refused her, some with even more contempt than Hanibal. The dark cloud of desperation that haunted Adaliah's dreams in the weeks since the fire now refused to be banished at the rising of the sun. The shadows clung to her every moment, closer than breath.

"Please." She extended the beautiful bowl again. "I have nowhere else to turn."

Anger stiffened his shoulders. "No, I tell you."

He slapped the bowl out of her hand and turned his back on her. The bowl fell to the hard-packed ground at her feet and broke in two.

Tears blurred her vision. Was there no one in all of Zarephath who would help her?

Danel sat cross-legged on the dirt beside Adaliah, watching as she milked Boz. Rather, as she attempted to milk Boz. She massaged the animal's shriveled udder to encourage milk to flow, but to no avail.

"I think that's all," Danel said.

Adaliah pulled the jug from beneath the goat and peered inside. There was barely enough for Danel to have a cup with his evening meal. For a week now the quantity of milk Boz produced had continued to dwindle, and Adaliah knew it was a matter of days before it stopped completely.

Boz turned her head and gave Adaliah a mournful look, as though to apologize for such a pitiful contribution. Adaliah patted the animal's side, noting the prominent rib cage. The grasses surrounding the village had been grazed all the way to the dry soil. The shepherd was forced to take the herd farther and farther into the plain and reported that even there the vegetation was brittle from lack of rain. A few local farmers had possessed the foresight to store hay in their barns, but they hoarded the bales as if they were made of gold. Several nights past, a man was caught trying to steal a bundle from a shed and had been whipped to death by the farmer and his sons. His death had been declared just, befitting his crime.

Or so Adaliah heard by listening to the women while waiting her turn at the well. Though she drew many covert glances, no one spoke to her directly unless it was to refuse to sell her food. She might as well have been a leper.

Aware of Danel's solemn gaze, she adopted a bright smile. "Let's see if we can find a carrot, shall we?"

In a small act of defiance she had watered her vegetables liberally, despite village leaders' warnings that the cisterns were emptying much too quickly. For the last few days she and Danel had unearthed one vegetable plant each day, though the time to harvest had not yet arrived. Even if grossly undersized, the potatoes, carrots, and onions complimented the bread and olives she served morning and evening.

She pointed out a plant, one of the few remaining, and Danel went to work digging to free the vegetable from the soil. As he did, she glanced up into the branches of the olive tree. Among the higher leaves she spied a few green olives. They wouldn't have time to ripen, but curing them in salt would draw out most of the bitterness.

"I got it."

With a triumphant grin he held up a carrot for her inspection. Adaliah smiled her approval, but inside her heart shrank. The puny thing was no longer than her son's hand. That stunted bit of produce wouldn't do much to fill a hungry child's belly.

Should they dig another? She conducted a quick inventory of the plants remaining in her garden. Two more carrots and two mounds that would yield four or six small potatoes each. Those, and a dozen unripe olives that would take days to cure. The grain jar was perhaps half full, which would last ten days at the most. Unless she made smaller loaves.

*I have to do something. But what?*

An idea came to her. If no one in Zarephath would sell her food, she would approach someone from another town.

She stood and picked up the milk jug. "Let's take a walk. I'd like to go down to the harbor."

Their feet kicked up dust on the steep path down the eastern side of the ridge separating Zarephath from the Great Sea. Even here the grass had dwindled to a few brown patches. They picked as much as they could find as they went along, to take back to Boz. Birds circled overhead, calling to one another in shrill voices.

They were in luck. A fishing boat was moored at the pier, and a trio of men were busy at the cleaning tables. Adaliah led Danel there.

The first man looked up at her approach, squinting against the sun. He acknowledged her with a nod, but his hands did not halt from their task of scraping scales from a fish the size of her arm.

She greeted him with a smile. "Good day to you."

"And to you." He flipped the fish over and began scraping that side.

"We've come to buy a fish." She set her basket on the dock and reached for her coin pouch.

"Have you, now?" His eyes narrowed further. "May I ask your name?"

Caution tingled along her spine. This was the same fisherman from whom she had purchased fish weeks ago, the awful day of the fire. He had not needed to know her name then.

"I am Adaliah, widow of Itthobaal the potter." She placed a hand on Danel's back. "And this is my son, Danel."

The man's gaze traveled from her to the child, and then he focused on his hands. "I've heard of you."

Though her insides quaked at the words, she froze her smile in place. "Have you?"

All scales removed, he tossed the cleaned fish into a bin at his feet and selected another one from a different bin. "I've been warned not to sell to you."

Her mouth went dry. "Warned? By whom?"

"Can't say." He whacked his knife down on the fish, severing its head with a powerful chop. A flick of the blade sent the head skittering off the side of the table onto a pile.

There was no use asking why. She glanced at Danel, who watched the exchange with a troubled expression, his brow furrowed with questions.

"Please." She took several coins from her pouch and extended them. "My son is hungry. Sell me a fish, and I promise no one will know."

His gaze strayed to the others on the dock. "Word has a way of getting around. If I sell to you, I won't sell a single fish to anyone in Zarephath ever again. The merchants will buy from another fishing boat, and I'll be out of business."

She ducked her head, trying to catch his eye, but he refused to look at her. Scales flew from the fish beneath the savage motions of his knife. Fighting tears, she dropped the coins back into her pouch. The entire village was against her, and now even those from other towns. Where could she turn? No one had spared her a kind word or a smile since the fire.

Except…

"There was a man here a few weeks ago, a Hebrew. He was carrying a load of wood toward the north harbor."

Though the fisherman's expression was as firmly shut as a barred door, he jerked a nod. "I know him. A boatbuilder. He left a few days ago for Tyre to deliver his boat."

Breath whooshed from her lungs, taking her hopes with it. Soaring above them, a gull cawed its mournful wail. She blinked tears from her eyes and watched it glide on the ocean's breeze. Was it too grieving a fruitless search for food?

Without warning, Danel dashed forward. He snatched a fish head from the pile at the man's feet, whirled, and scampered away.

"Hey!" The fisherman's angry bellow followed him, and he raised his knife above his head in a threatening manner.

Stunned, Adaliah watched her son race up the trail.

The man spat a curse after him. "That little thief." He turned a glare on her. "Raising him to be a criminal, are you? You should take him to a big city where he can practice snatching coin purses from old women."

She could find no answer to the charge. At that moment Danel did, indeed, resemble a youthful street urchin she'd once seen in Sidon who stole a pomegranate from a merchant's stall and dashed into the crowd to escape. Mumbling an offer to pay for the fish head—which was refused with a scowl—she grabbed her basket and hurried after her son.

Fish head soup wasn't nearly as distasteful as Adaliah feared it would be. Thin, to be sure, but she used sea salt and the last dried leaves of coriander to season the broth. A chopped carrot gave the dish a bit of texture.

"This is good." Danel lowered his bowl and smiled at her across the mat, his lips wet with soup.

She tore a piece of bread from the small cake she'd made for herself and moistened it in her own bowl. "Danel, we must talk about what happened at the harbor today."

He lowered his eyes and nodded.

"You know it's wrong to steal."

His lips pressed together to form a defiant line that reminded her sharply of his father. "I was hungry."

"I understand, but—"

"That man was mean." Anger rasped in the childish voice. She'd never heard that tone from him. "And he was going to throw the heads into the sea. I saw another fisherman do it, so I know he was."

Her heart twisted in her chest. So now they were reduced to scavenging scraps from garbage heaps. Shame sent a flood of heat into her face. Though she would never admit it, she knew she would have done the same if she'd thought of it first.

She cleared her throat. "That may be, but you mustn't take anything from anyone without asking first. If you had asked, he may have given us the scraps."

He clearly disagreed. His eyebrows crashed together in a stubborn scowl, but he remained silent.

"After today," she went on, "he won't look kindly on us. If we go back there again he won't look away. He might even chase us off the pier."

The scowl dissolved, replaced by a shamefaced frown. "I didn't think of that," he confessed.

She leaned across the mat and placed a hand on his arm. When he looked up, she held his gaze. "We will be fine. The gods will see to it." She paused. Did she believe that? No. The gods had not seen fit to send rain on the parched land. What evidence was there that they would offer any assistance to a woman and a hungry child? "*I* will see to it."

He subjected her to a long, searching gaze, and then nodded.

With a comforting smile that she didn't feel, she straightened. "Good. Now finish your soup and then go give Boz some water from the cistern jar."

"Yes, Imma."

When he had gone, Adaliah sat on her cushion for a long time, her thoughts chasing each other in circles. She couldn't encourage her son to steal. But his theft had been rewarded by providing their evening's meal. He might be tempted to do it again, only the next time where would he go? To the marketplace, like the young thief in Sidon? Or to the trash heaps of the people of Zarephath? And if he was caught, what would become of him? The fate of the man who'd tried to steal a bale of hay provided the terrifying answer.

No. She would not let that happen to her son. They had one ready source of food left to them, one she'd shied away from considering. But now she had no choice.

Late that night Adaliah lay on her sleeping pallet listening to her son's soft, even breathing. Her stomach quaked at the task that lay before her, but the time had come. She didn't want Danel to wake before she was finished.

Moving as quietly as she could, she rose and crept to the doorway of the bedchamber. She slipped through the curtain and let it fall shut behind her. From one of the shelves above her worktable she picked up the longest, sharpest knife she owned.

Moonlight reflected off the blade when she stepped outside. She tested the edge with a thumb. Itthobaal had always kept the knives sharpened, yet another thing she would have to learn to do herself. But not tonight, thank the gods.

Boz bleated softly at her approach. Tears pricked behind her eyes, but she refused to give in to them. She rested a hand on the goat's head for a moment, gathering her nerve.

"I'm sorry," she whispered in the moment before her knife did its work.

# CHAPTER EIGHT

At dawn Adaliah tossed the last bit of soil onto Boz's grave. It had been a long, messy task, but she calculated that she had enough meat on the drying racks to feed them for at least four weeks. Under normal circumstances that amount of meat would last much longer, but if she had nothing else to supplement their meals, the portions would need to be bigger.

The aroma of roasting meat had begun to waft from the pit. Though she regretted the lack of seasonings, tonight's meal would seem like a feast. And at least salt was plentiful this close to the ocean.

She was in the house grinding grain for the day's bread when the door opened and Tanytha entered carrying a water jug.

Without preamble, she announced, "I came to get Abba's bowls."

Danel, seated on his cushion waiting for the morning meal, eyed her warily. Adaliah's hands tightened on the grinding stone, but she continued her work.

"Do you mean my bowls?" she asked without looking up.

From the corner of her eye she saw Tanytha stiffen. "My abba made them, and I want them. You only want to sell them."

Adaliah acknowledged the statement with a nod. "But it seems no one wants to buy them. Odd, since they are beautifully crafted."

She glanced up and saw Tanytha's smirk. Anger erupted in her, and she attacked the grain with renewed force.

"How long before you realize you're not wanted here?" Tanytha's gaze slid from Adaliah to Danel, who watched the exchange with wide eyes. "Neither of you."

Adaliah slapped the grinding stone down. The thump made Danel jump.

She forced a smile and spoke softly to him. "I need more wood to cook our bread. Would you fetch some from the pile outside?"

With a cautious glance at Tanytha, he obeyed.

When he was out of earshot Adaliah rounded on Tanytha. "Is it not enough that you have turned everyone against us? Must you spew your poison in our home as well?"

Adaliah had never spoken with such force within Tanytha's hearing. Had Itthobaal been alive, such a display would have earned her a beating. Surprise sprang onto Tanytha's features. Surprise, and perhaps a touch of respect as well.

A moment later it was gone, replaced by a glare. "This was my home before it was yours. I won't rest until it is mine again."

Adaliah set her teeth together. "I won't let you take my son's inheritance."

Tanytha opened her mouth to reply but then closed it again. She sniffed and then narrowed her eyes. "What are you cooking?"

A breeze carried the aroma from the courtyard roasting pit through the open door.

With grim satisfaction, Adaliah replied, "Our evening meal."

"Where did *you* get meat?" Tanytha's lips twisted. "You must have stolen it."

Adaliah stiffened her spine. "I am not a thief."

At that moment Danel came through the courtyard door, his expression full of concern. "Imma, Boz is not here. Has she gone to graze with the shepherd?"

She hesitated. Throughout the night she'd planned how to explain her decision to Danel, but she didn't want to have that conversation in front of Tanytha.

The silence was broken by Tanytha's scornful laugh.

"I suppose you didn't steal the meat after all." A sneer curled her lips. "Enjoy your evening meal." She left the house laughing.

"For years Boz fed us with her milk," Adaliah told Danel as they walked side by side through the wheat field. "Now she is feeding us with her meat."

The child remained silent, his head lowered on the pretext of looking for unharvested grain. His shoulders slumped forward, and he shuffled his feet. She slowed her pace to match his.

"Do you understand why it was needed?" she asked.

He nodded and then bent down to pluck a few kernels from a stalk. When he dropped them into the jar she carried, he looked up into her face.

"I understand," he told her, his expression solemn. "But I will miss her."

A sorrowful lump gathered in her throat. "I will too."

They continued in silence to the edge of the field, stopping only twice more to add to the grain jar. On the opposite side, a movement attracted her attention. A man emerged from the landowner's house. He headed toward them, his stride long and purposeful. Though he was too far away for Adaliah to see his expression, his stiff posture warned her that they were about to be driven off. Long ago her grandmother had told her about Yahweh's instructions to the Hebrew people, allowing the poor to glean the fields after the harvest. She'd selected this field because of its distance from the village, in hopes that the owner either wouldn't notice them or wouldn't care if they picked up the remains. From the looks of him, she had been wrong.

"It's time to go," she told Danel.

He peered into the jar. "We didn't get very much."

"There isn't very much to get," she told him.

That was true. This man's workers had been thorough with the harvest.

As they left the field Adaliah glanced behind them. The landowner had stopped and stood with his hands planted on his hips, watching their retreat.

At home she added the grain to her dwindling supply and then took Danel up to the roof to check the drying racks. She showed him how to turn the strips of meat so the sun would dry them evenly, and then left him to the task while she added wood to the fire on top of the roasting pit.

"Hello," a voice called.

She straightened and turned to find Tanytha's husband standing in the doorway of the house. Though she had always liked Resheph, his appearance so soon after the heated encounter with Tanytha made her cautious. Had he come to reprimand her for speaking harshly to his wife?

But he gave them both a pleasant smile. "I knocked on the door but then heard your voices out here."

"I'm curing meat in the sun," Danel called down from the roof with an air of importance.

"And doing a fine job of it, I'm sure." He faced Adaliah. "I hoped to have a word with you."

She searched his face but saw no reprimand lurking there. "Let's go inside."

Danel stayed to finish his chore while Adaliah led Resheph into the house. He sat on a cushion while she filled a cup with cool water.

"It's a good thing we have a deep well," he said when she handed it to him. "At the rate the cisterns are emptying we'll have to start using well water for everything soon."

She seated herself across the mat from him. "I hope it doesn't dry up from lack of rain."

He drank from the cup and then held it in one hand. From the folds of his outer tunic he took a small pouch.

"Dried apples," he said as he extended it to her. "I know Danel likes them."

Tears sprang to her eyes at the unexpected gift. Embarrassed, she dashed them away.

"That's very kind. Thank you."

He looked uncomfortable and then blurted, "Tanytha doesn't know I brought them."

The comment held an unspoken request.

"I won't say anything," she promised.

For a long moment neither of them spoke. Adaliah watched him toy with the cup, turning it in his hands. He appeared to be hesitant to speak his mind and avoided her eye.

"Is your family well?" she asked.

"Yes. Uday's wife is expected to give birth soon."

She hadn't realized his brother was expecting another child. Their third, if she remembered correctly. No doubt that played into Tanytha's cruel behavior. Resheph's brother and his family also lived in their father's home, so Tanytha faced a daily reminder of her barrenness.

"That is what I wanted to talk to you about," he said.

"Your brother's child?"

"Uday is filling the house with offspring. Farah does not treat Tanytha well. My mother is constantly having to settle arguments between them."

A difficult position, to be sure. No doubt Resheph felt torn between his wife and the other women of his family. That, plus Tanytha's tendency to shrewishness, and the poor man in front of her probably led a fairly miserable life at his father's home. But what did that have to do with—

Realization dawned on Adaliah. "You want me to move back to Sidon and give my house to Tanytha so you can move out of your father's home."

"No." He leaned forward and set his cup on the mat. "I want you to move back to Sidon and sell me the house and the kiln."

Disappointment struck her at his words, though why she thought Resheph would side with her over his wife she didn't know. The gift of dried apples, perhaps. But that gesture had been designed to put her off guard, to make her consider his offer favorably.

When she didn't answer immediately, he continued.

"I have arranged to hire a skilled potter from Tyre who will come to Zarephath and teach me the potter's craft. Itthobaal's family business will continue."

"What of *your* family's business?"

"Uday is better suited. Like my father, he takes great satisfaction in producing dozens of shades of purple." He waved a hand in a gesture of dismissal. "Let him slave over the stinking mollusks, extracting their dye."

"How do you know you'll like working at a potter's wheel any better? You have never done it," she pointed out.

"But I have," he said. "Itthobaal had begun to teach me before he died. He intended to take me on as an apprentice and train me to take over one day."

Adaliah stiffened. Was that true? She'd heard nothing about the matter. But Itthobaal was not in the habit of confiding his plans to her.

"What of Danel?" Her voice sounded sharper than she intended.

"We would have worked it out." He waved his hand again, this time in a vague gesture that did not put her at ease.

Abruptly, Adaliah stood. Under the pretext of storing the apples in a jar on the shelf, she turned her back on him. Whatever agreement he and Itthobaal had made, she was under no obligation to honor it.

On the other hand, maybe this could work to her advantage.

Gathering her nerve, she turned to face him. "The kiln will one day be Danel's. I won't sell it." Resheph drew breath to answer, but she held up a hand. "But I will allow you to use it to learn the skill *if* your hired potter trains Danel too."

His eyes narrowed. "And what of the house?"

She shook her head. "It is not for sale."

A series of emotions marched across his face. Dismay. Impatience. Resignation. And the one that remained, anger.

"I hoped you would see reason, but I suppose you really are as obstinate as Tanytha claims." His mouth a hard slash, he got to his feet. "If I'm not to have Itthobaal's kiln and my wife is not to have his house, then I'm not inclined to train your son."

"Itthobaal's son," she reminded him.

He shrugged. "You will both be much better off in Sidon."

"So I hear," she replied, her voice cool. "Constantly."

He headed toward the door but stopped before pushing it open.

"I can't help but wonder something." He caught her eye and held it. "Why didn't you call for help when your husband was trapped? I'm beginning to think Tanytha has the right of it. It's almost as if you wanted him to die."

Her head went light as blood drained from her face. With a final rigid smile, he left.

Adaliah took a backward step and leaned against the work-table for support. With his parting words, Resheph's jab landed true. When Itthobaal lay screaming at her to help him, she had hesitated. Because she hated him. Shame burned in her stomach, searing her mind with the ugly truth. She caused his death as surely as if she had set the fire with her own hands.

A noise in the night brought Adaliah out of a fitful sleep. She lay on her pallet, her ears straining to hear the sound repeated. Danel slept on beside her, undisturbed. Had the noise come from inside the house? Fear rendered her motionless, her heart pounding in her ears.

When minutes stretched by with no repeat of the sound, she forced herself to relax. No one was in her house. She and Danel were safe. She closed her eyes and tried to go back to sleep.

Some time later she gave up. Her mind was too alert, her thoughts too turbulent. She rose and, taking care not to wake Danel, slipped out of the bedchamber.

White moonlight filtered through the open window in the back of the house. The fire in her cooking grate had burned down to a few glowing embers still glowing in the midst of the ashes. She considered lighting a lamp but decided against the idea. Instead she opened the courtyard door and crept outside.

The cool night air carried the salty smell of the sea. She climbed the stairs to the roof and then shut her eyes and listened to the sound of the waves in the distance, willing them to soothe her troubled thoughts. How often since her marriage had she risen in the night, leaving Itthobaal snoring on his mat, to enjoy a moment of peace? Even Boz seemed to recognize her need for solitude and would nicker softly as if in comfort.

Regret washed over her at the reminder. She opened her eyes to look down in the courtyard, toward the mound where the goat's carcass was buried—

And gasped.

The drying racks were gone. Someone had stolen their meat.

A black pit of despair opened in her soul.

# CHAPTER NINE

**M**orning found her winding through the streets of Zarephath, her steps determined and her mood grim. Before her lay a loathsome task, but she had no choice. Trying to hold on to her house and the kiln was making her and Danel's lives miserable, maybe even putting them in jeopardy. Her desire to secure her son's future livelihood was leading them down a path to disaster.

But she would *not* give Tanytha the victory. She'd burn her house to the ground like Itthobaal's shop rather than see that spiteful woman living there.

Though the sun had barely risen above the horizon, Badahur's workshop buzzed with activity. Young men sat at three pottery benches, the sound of their feet kicking the wheel creating a rhythmic beat to the whir of the plates. A fourth bent over a low table in the back, intent on carving a design into a large platter. They all looked up when she stepped through the door.

She cast a quick glance around the shop. "I'm here to see Badahur."

The one carving answered. "You'll find him out back, at the kiln." He lifted his tool and pointed toward the rear door, which stood open.

Thanking him, she wound her way through the shop, noting several shelves stacked with dull gray bowls, cups, and pitchers waiting to be glazed.

The smell of smoke struck her when she stepped outside. With it, the memory of the choking cloud from which she had pulled Danel rushed back to her. And then a vivid image of Itthobaal, lying beneath the shelf, his temple bloody.

*"Where are you, you worthless wretch? Help me!"*

Her eyelids shut of their own accord, but once again, she could not escape the image seared into her mind's eye.

"Look who has come to visit."

A haughty voice pulled her out of the memory. She opened her eyes to find Badahur and a young man standing in front of the cave-like kiln, watching her. The boy held an armload of wood, and behind them the door to the kiln's firebox stood open. Flames flickered from within its shallow depths.

"It's Zarephath's newest kiln owner." A sneer twisted Badahur's lips. "The widow of Zarephath."

She steeled herself against the taunt. It would only hurt her cause if she became angry.

"May I have a moment of your time?" she asked in as calm a tone as she could manage.

He studied her for a long moment and then jerked a nod. Then he seemed to become aware of the boy, who stood beside him, gawking at her. He slapped the back of the lad's head with a harsh, flat-handed blow.

"What are you doing? Get busy. That fire won't build itself."

The boy whirled toward the firebox and began feeding logs into the flames.

Badahur folded his arms across his chest and leveled a stare on her. "Well? What do you want?"

Adaliah glanced around. She'd prefer to conduct this conversation in private, not out in the open where they could be overheard. But the only person she saw in the area was the boy.

She straightened and looked Badahur in the eye. "I've reconsidered your offer."

A slow smile spread across his face, and not a pleasant one. The sight of it stirred feelings of discomfort to life in her.

"Have you, now?"

"Yes. I will sell you my kiln."

A corner of his mouth curled upward. "At a high price, I imagine."

Through the long early-morning hours, she had given careful consideration to the price she would ask. The truth was she had no idea of the value of any kiln, much less one of the quality Itthobaal's seemed to have. The money would have to last her and Danel for quite a while, until she found some industry that could support them. But money was a secondary consideration. What she needed the most was his support.

"You name the price," she told him, and had the satisfaction of seeing his eyebrows shoot upward toward his hairline. "I trust you to be fair."

The last was a lie, but what choice did she have?

She continued. "In addition to the price for the kiln, I ask that you make it known throughout the village that my son and

I have your patronage. I want to be treated in an equitable manner, the same as any other Sidonese woman."

He made no immediate answer. He raised one hand and began to pluck at his beard while he subjected her to a calculating stare.

"You want me to become your benefactor."

Though the statement was not a question, she nodded in answer. With an effort she managed to stand still before him, her shoulders stiff and her spine erect. Inside, she cringed away from his shrewd expression.

Finally, he dropped his hand. "I've changed my mind. I no longer wish to buy your kiln."

Breath left her lungs in a rush. "But you said—"

He held up a hand. "I know what I said, but as you pointed out, the kiln is old. I can refit one of mine with metal supports if I want."

Despite the sun's morning rays and the heat wafting from the firebox in front of her, Adaliah's face felt cold, bloodless. She had not considered the possibility of Badahur changing his mind.

Gathering her nerve, she took a step toward him. "Please. I beg of you. Even if you don't buy the kiln, give me your patronage. Let it be known that you support a poor widow and her son."

Standing this close, he towered over her. Her eyes were on level with his shoulder, and she had to crane her neck to look up into his face. His size frightened her. She clasped her hands together to keep them still.

A change came over him then. The chill in his eyes warmed, replaced by a flicker of something that made her flesh crawl. She'd seen that expression often enough from Itthobaal to know what it meant.

"Since you beg so prettily, perhaps we can reach an agreement." He lifted his hand and rested it on her shoulder. "You're not unattractive, and still young. Young enough to bear more sons."

A desert invaded her mouth. She opened it to voice a protest but could only manage a squeak.

He laughed, a low chuckle that rumbled in his chest. "Here's a new offer. Become my wife. You and your son will be fed, and the only thing you'll have to worry about is keeping me happy." His fingers slipped inside the neck of her tunic to massage the tender skin there.

"B-but you have a wife already." Didn't he?

"I have three. You would be the fourth." He leaned closer, so close his breath warmed her cold cheeks. "Have no fear. I can take care of four."

A shudder ripped through her body. "And what of my house? My kiln?"

"They would become mine upon our marriage, of course." His hand tightened, squeezing her neck so firmly she cried out. "Think about it. You won't get a better offer."

With a shove, he pushed her away, and she stumbled backward. Then he turned his back on her and began berating the boy for not setting the wood appropriately in the firebox.

Adaliah regained her balance, her hands covering the sore place on her neck. Sobs gathered in the base of her throat, but she swallowed hard against them. As a fourth wife she would occupy the lowest place in the family structure. The other wives would probably resent her. Her son would become little more than Badahur's slave. She couldn't do that to him. Or to herself.

Tears threatened to blind her, but she braced herself against them. If she gave in to her sorrow now, she might never be able to stop. Besides, she did have one option left.

Turning, she stumbled in the direction of the temple. She would spend a few precious coins to pay a scribe to write a letter to her father in Sidon.

The priest's scribe set his sharpened reed on the surface of the table, straightened, and blew on the ink through pursed lips. Standing before him, Adaliah inspected the neat figures scrawled across the papyrus. She recognized a few of the symbols and knew their meanings, thanks to her father's tutelage when she was younger, but the task of writing an entire letter was far beyond her skills.

Satisfied that the ink was dry, the bare-faced man picked up the missive and held it up. Scars covered his arms, some of them fresh from recent worship ceremonies. A lock of hair had escaped its binding as he worked, and this he absently pushed away from his face as he read the letter aloud.

*To Damos son of Zafir. Your daughter, Adaliah, sends to greet you and those of your house. I bless you to Baal, Lady Ashtoreth, and all the gods of Sidon. May they guard you and keep you well.*

Adaliah hid a smile as she imagined Father's reaction to the standard salutation. He cared little for the gods and placed no store in their blessings, a sentiment shared by his daughter.

*I write this missive with a heavy heart. My husband is dead from a fire that destroyed his pottery workshop. Thanks be to the gods our son was rescued and is alive, but our straits are dire. I have no livelihood, no means to provide for us. The drought that plagues this land has robbed me of even the ability to grow food to supply our meager needs.*

*For that reason, I beg leave to return to your home if you will have us. Your grandson has recently passed the fourth anniversary of his birth and is a capable child. He is eager to learn a trade and is old enough to be of help to you at the looms.*

*Preparations for our journey north will not take long. We will set out as soon as we receive your permission. Father, please reply with all haste. Our situation grows more desperate each day.*

*Written by Cali, scribe-priest of Baal, and sealed by my own hand.*

He raised an inquiring look to her. When she nodded, he set the letter down in front of her, dipped the reed in the ink pot, and handed it to her.

Adaliah took the writing instrument and, with painstaking care, inscribed the symbols that spelled her name. When she lifted the reed from the parchment, ink dripped from the sharpened tip. A black blot besmirched the last symbol. Dismayed, she looked up at the priest.

He inspected the letter, his lips curled with disdain. "If I have to write it a second time it will cost you double."

Though she hated sending a blotched letter, she could not afford to part with more of her precious stash of coins. Besides the scribe's fee, she would have to pay a courier to deliver the missive.

"This will be fine," she told him.

But as he rolled the papyrus, that black blot hovered in her mind's eye. She couldn't rid herself of the idea that the blot on the letter somehow portended the failure of yet another of her plans.

# CHAPTER TEN

On his hands and knees, Danel studied the mat where Imma served their meals, searching for crumbs. A rumble in his stomach seemed to rip through the silence in the house. The morning was only half spent, and already hunger gnawed at his belly. The mat was clean, all the crumbs already found and devoured.

He sat back on his heels and eyed the shelf where Imma stored food in jars made by his abba. There were olives in the brown jar, he knew. And grain in the red one, and oil in the one with the spout that had been stained the color of the Great Sea. Wrapped in an oiled cloth was a chunk of roasted meat—an image of Boz rose in his mind, but his thoughts skittered away from the painful conclusion—left over from last night's meal. But he dared not touch any of these. When Imma came home from her errand she would know, and while she might not be angry with him, she would look sad. He didn't want to see sorrow replace the special smile she reserved just for him.

Resigned, he got to his feet and climbed the narrow stairway leading to the upstairs room that had been his. It was warmer up here, though the shutters on both windows were left open to catch the breeze. His sleeping pallet lay in one corner, unused since Abba's death. The hooks on the wall were bare, since Imma had moved his tunics downstairs. But the stool still sat before the window. Many nights he had sat on that stool, long after Imma and Abba thought he was asleep, and counted the stars. There were a bunch of them twinkling against a canopy of blue so deep it looked almost black. Once he got past twenty, he had trouble keeping track, and his lack of counting skill frustrated him. One day he would know everything there was to know about the stars.

And making pots, he supposed. That's what Abba told him he would do when he became a man, though the day he'd spent at the shop had held little appeal for him. He didn't tell Abba, but the clay felt like a mushy lump beneath his fingers, and from the moment he touched it, he itched to wash it off. But he wanted his abba to be proud of him, even in the afterlife. And someday Danel would need to make money to buy food for his imma. So he would make pots.

Maybe he could carve star designs in them.

The emptiness of the room was depressing. He descended the stairs to the courtyard and went to the mound of earth beneath which Imma had buried the parts of Boz that weren't meat. He stood looking down at the soil.

"I miss you."

Heaving a sigh, he went to the jug where they kept cistern water and poured a dipperful onto each plant in the garden. Two carrots, two potatoes.

After he returned the dipper to the jug, he stood before the statue of the Baal. Bracing himself, he raised his gaze to look into the face. This statue had always terrified him. The stony eyes glared, and the pointed horns on its head looked like weapons. And that lightning bolt…he shuddered. Did the king of the gods really look like that? If so, Danel hoped he would never have to meet him.

He started to turn away, but something stopped him. What was that on top of the god's head? A patch of white, directly between the horns. He drew closer and rose on his toes to peer at it.

Then a smile broke out on his face. Bird poop! Baal had poop on his head. The idea of a mighty god, the leader of all the gods, letting a bird poop on his head like that seemed so silly it made him laugh. Why would a mighty god stand for such treatment? Danel laughed and laughed, doubling over and holding his empty stomach until the laughter dissolved into an amused chuckle.

A thought occurred to him. If Baal was so powerful, as the priests said, why did he allow such shameful treatment of himself? Why didn't the poop miraculously disappear from his head, and the bad bird die with a lightning bolt through its body?

If Baal was so powerful, why did he let Abba die in a fire? Why did he make Imma cry in the night when she thought Danel couldn't hear? Why didn't he send them some food? Danel's stomach rumbled as if to emphasize the question.

There were only two reasons he could think of. Either Baal wasn't as powerful as the priests claimed, or he didn't care about them. Probably he didn't care. Gods didn't have time to think about poor people, no matter how the priests jumped around and cut themselves until blood dripped from their fingers.

But Baal wasn't the only god. There were others, gods and goddesses who might be kinder. One day, when Danel was older, he would find out about all the gods. Then he would choose to worship one who was nicer, one who cared about poor boys and their immas.

With a daring kick at the idol's knee, Danel ran into the house.

# CHAPTER ELEVEN

Adaliah picked up a charred board and peered beneath it. Nothing but soot. Gulping against a lump in her throat, she let it fall back into place. What had happened to Itthobaal's coin chest?

She straightened and pressed her fist into an ache in the small of her back. Above her the sun rode high in the sky, its unsympathetic rays shining onto the ash-covered remains of Itthobaal's shop. When she was gone Resheph would probably replace the roof and clear away the charred remnants of Itthobaal's business. He would have to buy a new pottery wheel and tools and—

With a stomp of her foot, she put a halt to those thoughts. She didn't care what Resheph did with the workshop after she and Danel left for Sidon. Nor did she care what Tanytha did with the house.

Well, not much.

If only Adaliah could find that chest.

A scratching noise drew her attention to the doorway, and she looked up to find Danel watching her. She'd left him at home, not wanting to subject him to another session of sifting through ash and soot. She opened her mouth, but the greeting died on her tongue unsaid. When had he become so gaunt? His cheekbones protruded sharply beneath the eyes she loved so well. When had those creases appeared on the tender skin of his forehead, leaving him with a perpetual look of worry and care?

She forced a smile. "I thought you were at home sleeping."

"A letter came from Sidon" he told her. "We need to go to the temple so the scribe can read it to us."

Her heartbeat sped with a jolt of excitement. It had only been four days since she sent the letter in the care of a wool merchant from Tyre who passed through the village on his way to Sidon. Father answered quickly, as she had requested.

"My father, your grandfather, has sent an answer."

He cocked his head sideways to give her a curious look. "An answer to what question?"

She hadn't told him of her decision, or about the letter she'd written to Father. The child had enough worries without fretting over the loss of his abba's business and the only home he'd ever known.

"You'll see." She infused her smile with enthusiasm. "Come. Let's go to the temple."

They stopped at the closest cistern along the way, where Adaliah washed her hands and face. Her clothing was covered in ash with black smears, but she didn't want to take time to change into her other tunic. Instead she hurried through the streets of Zarephath, Danel trotting to keep pace with her.

At the temple she went to the side door, the one where the scribes worked. A blue-robed priest, older than the one who had penned her letter, sat on a stool at a worktable, his attention focused on a scroll. He looked up when they entered, and his gaze traveled the length of her soiled tunic. His expression became one of disdain.

Adaliah dipped her head in a gesture of respect. "Forgive my appearance. I was working when a messenger arrived with news of a letter."

Heaving a heavy sigh that let her know he wasn't pleased with the interruption to his studies, he rolled up the scroll. "You are Adaliah, widow of Itthobaal?" At her nod, he told her, "Wait here."

He disappeared through a doorway behind him. She gave Danel a reassuring smile, tapping her fingers on her thigh impatiently. Unbeknownst to Danel, she had already begun preparations for their move to Sidon. She'd sorted through their meager possessions, selecting which items would travel with them and which she would leave behind. The wool merchant who carried her letter to Father mentioned an acquaintance who would follow him soon, and she planned to ask if they could accompany him. If not, or if he tarried too long, she would spend the last of her money to buy a wheeled cart, and she and Danel would make the journey by themselves.

The priest returned, a rolled papyrus in his hand. He seated himself again on his stool before extending it toward her.

"Would you read it to us?" she asked.

The corners of his lips curved upward. "I will, for two *gerah*." He held out a hand.

Biting her tongue at the high price, Adaliah fumbled with her pouch and extracted the coins. Her money was rapidly disappearing, but what did that matter, as long as she had enough to see them safely to Father's house?

After pocketing the coins, the priest unrolled the papyrus and smoothed it out on the table.

*To Adaliah, widow of Itthobaal, from Marte, wife of Tavis the carpet weaver.*

At the opening words, Adaliah felt a chill creep over her as the blood seeped from her face. Why didn't Father answer her letter? Why did he leave the task to her sister, Marte?

The priest looked up at her, his lips twisted with disapproval. "She does not include a blessing, or the mention of any gods."

Adaliah remained mute, her tongue too numb to utter a reply.

With a sigh, he continued. *"It is with great sadness that I tell you of the passing of our father. Two harvests have gone by since he caught the ague and died five days later."*

A sickening dizziness came over Adaliah, and she stepped forward to grip the edge of the worktable to keep from falling. The priest continued as if he did not notice.

*"My husband, Tavis, now runs the looms, as our father taught him. Our sons work alongside him, and together they have enough trade to keep them busy. There is no place in the business for your son, and no room for you in our house."* The priest's expression brightened. "Here is the blessing, at the end. *Entrust your lives to the*

*gods. Perhaps they will take pity on you. Written by Tavis, son of Omri, and sealed by my own hand."*

He held the papyrus out to her. "Sound advice, to appeal to the gods."

Dazed, Adaliah took the letter from his hand. He unrolled his scroll and returned to his reading while she stood staring at the symbols at the bottom of the letter. Marte's name, taught to her by Father, just as he had taught Adaliah. They had never been close. Marte had always resented her because their mother died in childbirth, and after an argument had once accused, "It's your fault she's dead. It should have been you." But that had been long ago, when they were both young. Now that they were grown, surely Marte didn't still blame her for killing their mother.

As Tanytha considered her to blame for killing her father.

A deep breath shuddered in her chest. *I am to blame for two deaths.*

Danel slipped his hand into hers. She looked down at him, and her heart clenched at the worry that twisted his young features. No words of comfort came to mind, but she smiled and squeezed his hand.

The priest lifted his gaze, his expression one of impatience. "Is there something else?"

Laughter threatened to escape her throat. *No, there is nothing else. I have no more ideas, nowhere else to turn.*

Marte's parting words, which Adaliah knew were not written in blessing but in contempt, came back to her. *Entrust your lives to the gods.* Adaliah had no more faith in gods than her sister did, but perhaps the gods' devoted servants could be moved to compassion by the plight of a starving widow and her son.

"Yes," she said, pleased when her voice came out strong. "I would like to see Fayez."

They were forced to wait until Fayez finished his priestly duties. When he joined them in the small chamber where the scribe-priest had left them, a raw odor that made Adaliah's stomach twitch invaded the room. His robes were wet with the blood of the sacrifice he'd just performed.

Fayez let the curtain fall shut behind him and then seated himself on a bench facing theirs. "I understand you've received bad news from Sidon."

Apparently the scribe-priest had told him the contents of Marte's letter. Grateful that she didn't have to speak the words, Adaliah nodded.

"May the gods speed your father's passage." He spoke the standard condolence by rote, his voice devoid of emotion. "What did you want to see me about?"

She clasped her hands together in her lap. "My situation—" With a quick smile at Danel beside her, she corrected herself. "Our situation has become desperate. We've fallen victim to lies, maltreatment, and even theft."

His expression did not change.

Gathering her courage, she continued. "We need your help. A word from you will set things right with the people."

"I told you before, I will tell anyone who asks that you were at the harbor buying fish when the fire broke out." He began tapping his foot impatiently against the floor.

"It isn't about that anymore. They're trying to drive us out of Zarephath, out of our home." She leaned forward and held his gaze. "Speak to Tanytha on our behalf. Convince her to stop this persecution."

"Do you think you are the only desperate person in Zarephath?" His mouth twisted. "If I involve myself in the petty affairs of one needy person, how long would it be before I am overrun with similar requests? The temple would drown in petitions for charity, and then who would conduct the ceremonies that appease the gods?"

A looming panic squeezed her throat tight. "I am not asking for charity. I'm asking to be treated justly."

Her voice filled the small chamber, distress giving it volume. Beside her on the bench, Danel scooted closer, his small body pressed against her side.

"Perhaps you should beg for charity," Fayez said. "Of course, beggars fare well in bigger cities than in towns the size of Zarephath."

The ice in his features sent a chill down her spine. What had she expected? That the chief priest would care about the plight of a widow, when the gods he served did not?

His forehead cleared, and he appeared to have a thought. "Perhaps you could appeal to the gods. If you make a worthy offering, they may be moved to act on your behalf."

She wanted to laugh. Where were the gods when she was taken away from her home by a cruel husband? Where were they when she sobbed quietly on her pallet, bleeding from Itthobaal's treatment? Where were they when Father died, or even when her mother died?

"The gods have never spared a thought for me," she told him. "I have no reason to believe they will now."

"Perhaps you have never given them anything they considered worthy enough." The frigid eyes moved from her to Danel.

Horror crept over her. Give Danel to the gods? Watch as the priest laid him on the altar, as the sacrificial knife descended, as his blood dripped into the chalice to be poured out at Baal's feet? Bile churned in her empty stomach.

She put her arm around her son and drew him close, her gaze fixed on Fayez. "I will die first," she whispered.

He smiled. "That too will serve their purpose."

Adaliah held firmly onto Danel's hand as they left the temple. Her insides churned with so many emotions she couldn't discern between them. Anger. Disgust. Alarm. Dread. And overriding all, fear so intense she could barely breathe. What options were left to her?

"Imma."

Danel tugged at her arm. She realized she had been striding across the plaza so quickly he was running to keep up with her. Contrite, she stopped and knelt before him.

"I'm sorry." Desperate tears invaded her voice, and she cleared her throat before going on. "I should have sent you home after we heard the letter. I—I thought the chief priest would be able to help. I didn't know he would…"

How much of Fayez's conversation had Danel understood? She spared a desperate hope that he had missed the meaning of that final suggestion.

"Everything will be all right."

He reached out to take her hand and patted it. The gesture was so adult that her heart twisted in her chest.

"Truly they will." She forced a confident smile for his benefit. "The gods may smile on us yet."

His expression grew solemn. "Do you really think so?"

It was an earnest question. A trite answer rose to her lips. *Of course, sweet boy. There's no need to worry.* But she couldn't force the words out. She shifted beneath his steady gaze as he waited for an answer. If she were to reply with complete honesty, she would say, *No. We can't rely on any gods, because they don't care.* But she couldn't make herself say that either. So she said nothing.

He gave a small nod, as though to say he understood. "I am small. I don't need much food."

Before he could see the tears that swam into her eyes, she grabbed him and pulled him into a fierce hug. There was still one avenue open to her. Much as she dreaded it, she had no choice but to accept Badahur's offer.

When she had composed herself, she released Danel. Smiling, she told him, "Go home. I'll be there soon."

She found Badahur in his shop. He stood over a young man who sat before the wheel as he molded the spinning lump of clay. He bore such a strong resemblance to Badahur he could be none other than his son. Adaliah judged him to be only a few years younger than herself.

Badahur's eyes narrowed when she entered. He examined her down the length of his nose, and she flushed. She'd forgotten about her soot-stained dress.

"What brings the widow of Zarepheth to my shop? Not here to buy my bowls, I'd wager."

His tone bit into her tender feelings, and she battled the tears that hovered so close to the surface lately.

"Could we speak privately?" she asked.

"I'm too busy to be bothered by arrogant widows today." He dismissed her with an impatient wave. "Off with you."

"Please." She extended a hand toward him. "I-I've come to accept your offer."

"I've told you once already, I'm no longer interested in buying your kiln."

"Not that offer." His eyebrows arched, and she stiffened her spine. "I accept your proposal of marriage."

The young man at the wheel missed a kick, and his mouth gaped open.

Badahur slapped the back of his head. "Pay attention." Then he looked up at Adaliah. "I've had time to reconsider.

What do I need with a fourth wife? Especially one whose last husband died under suspicious circumstances."

The words rang in her ears. Her head felt light. *This cannot be happening.*

"But you'll gain not only a wife but also my kiln. And my house." She gulped a shuddering breath. "And it will cost you nothing."

"Nothing except two more mouths to feed and another whining brat to raise. Besides"—his expression became shrewd—"I heard you were returning to your father's house."

Her head dropped forward as a fresh wave of grief washed over her. "My father is dead."

For a moment she thought the news might move him. If pity was the only emotion she could stir in him, so be it.

He remained silent and cocked his head sideways as he studied her. "That is unfortunate. But I have a suggestion." He crossed the few steps between them to stand directly in front of her, forcing her to look up at him. "You could go into temple service. There is a place for women like you at the temple of Asherah." He ran a finger down her arm. "I'd even come to worship with you there."

Bile rose into her throat. Rubbing her arm to calm the crawling flesh, she whirled. His laughter followed her into the street.

# CHAPTER TWELVE

**B**rook Kerith had become no more than a thin trail of mud that extended the length of the ravine. Elijah sat on the hillside with his back against a tree trunk, watching a long-eared hare attempt to suck moisture from the damp soil. Yesterday Elijah had been able to drink a mouthful by wrapping mud in the hem of his robe and squeezing a drizzle of water into his mouth. Today the same procedure had yielded only a few drops. And still, the end of the drought had not yet come, nor would it for some time. The Lord had revealed to him that the rains would not fall, nor the dew refresh the land, for many more months.

Elijah's time in this valley was coming to an end. He felt that in his soul, though Yahweh remained consistently vague regarding timing. Still, Elijah occasionally liked to ask.

"How much longer, Lord God?"

At the sound of his voice, the hare scurried away.

*Now.*

The answer resonated throughout Elijah's being, deeper than his bones, bringing with it the certainty of divine guidance. Laughing, he got to his feet. Perhaps Yahweh had been waiting for him to voice the question again.

"And where am I going?"

Though he would gladly travel to Samaria to face Ahab and even Jezebel if it would mean an end to this drought, Elijah knew that wasn't the Lord's plan. Not yet.

*Go at once to Zarephath in the region of Sidon and stay there.*

His jaw went slack, and he lifted his head to search the cloudless sky above him. Sidon, the Phoenician center of pagan worship, and where Jezebel's own father ruled. Did Yahweh have a warning for King Ethbaal, perhaps? Unlikely, since few Israelites lived in Sidon.

Though King Ahab might travel there to meet with his ally and father-in-law, perhaps accompanied by his wicked queen. Maybe Yahweh would arrange a meeting whereby Elijah would deliver another warning to Israel's king to turn from his idolatrous ways.

"Am I to prophesy in Zarephath?" he asked.

*I have directed a widow there to supply you with food.*

Not to prophesy, then, but to shelter there. Laughter rumbled in Elijah's chest, and he let it fill the air around him. Yahweh was planning to hide His prophet beneath Jezebel's very nose.

Still chuckling, he tightened the straps on his sandals and left the valley that had been his home for the past few months.

# CHAPTER THIRTEEN

Adaliah sliced the last olive in two while Danel watched. She pushed a piece across the platter.

"Yours is smaller," he said in a flat tone.

"My potato is bigger." She pointed to the halved vegetable, also their last.

He opened his lips, apparently ready to argue the fact, but instead heaved a long sigh. The fear that had taken up permanent residence in the depths of her soul pushed its way to the fore at the look of resignation on her son's face. The purplish skin beneath his eyes darkened with each passing day, and his shoulder bones protruded sharply beneath his threadbare tunic.

They ate their meager meal in silence, washing it down with plenty of water. At least Adaliah had not been banned from the well, though she had taken to filling her jar late at night when there was little chance that she would meet anyone. The sight of their arrogant stares and whispers would have once made her angry, but now she had no energy to spare on fits of temper.

Danel emptied his cup and got to his feet. He bent down to reach for the platter, but Adaliah picked it up first.

"I'll take care of this," she told him. "You can go gather wood for tonight's fire."

He started to turn but then stopped. "Can I do it later? I'm tired. I want to lie down."

She started to protest that he had risen only a short while ago, but his arms hung limply at his sides and his eyelids drooped with exhaustion. Despair pressed in on her so tightly she could barely breathe. Her son was dying, starving to death right before her eyes. And she was helpless to stop it.

"Later will be fine."

She put the tray on her worktable, wiped the cups with her apron, and set them on the shelf with the others. Her fingers brushed the grain jar. After taking it down, she peered inside. Only a handful of grain remained, and a few drops of oil in the jug. Enough for two small cakes of bread for their evening meal.

She replaced the jar then wandered around the living chamber looking for something to occupy her time. Finding nothing, she went out to the courtyard. Her garden was full of dry soil and holes from where she and Danel had dug yesterday in hopes of finding a stray vegetable they might have missed. Her gaze strayed to a larger hole beyond, where she had unearthed Boz's carcass a few days past. Though she'd cut the decayed places away as best she could, the broth she'd made of the bones tasted of rot and dirt. They had choked it down anyway, and then vomited half the night. The effort had left them weaker than before with no means of regaining their strength.

She turned, and her gaze fell on the statue of Baal. Its sightless eyes no longer frightened her. How could they, when she didn't believe in a god who could not see the plight of innocent people—or chose not to see? If gods existed at all, they kept to themselves and left mortals to their own devices.

*What of Yahweh?*

The question surprised her. She hadn't thought of her grandmother's God since that day in the field, when she and Danel had been gleaning for unharvested grain. If Grandmother was right, the Hebrew God not only concerned Himself with human conditions, but decreed mandates for the care of widows and orphans.

Adaliah closed her eyes and searched her memory for the stories she learned at Grandmother's knee. How the Hebrew God formed a man with His own hands and gave him life. How He gave that man a woman so he wouldn't be lonely and fed them both from His own beautiful garden.

A humorless laugh escaped her lips. If only that God would feed her and Danel from His garden, like those first people.

*Ask.*

The word appeared in her mind as if placed there by someone other than herself. She put a hand to her neck and massaged the tight muscles there. How could she ask Yahweh for anything when He had no presence in the temple in Zarephath? Grandmother had told her that Yahweh had His own temple in Jerusalem, far south of here. Adaliah had no way of getting there, and if she did, she had no offering to make so Yahweh would look with favor on her request.

*Ask now.*

She looked around. No one was in sight. What harm could it do to voice a request to an invisible, and probably nonexistent,

God? She turned her back on the dead eyes of the statue and spoke in the direction of the olive tree.

"Yahweh." Try though she might, she could not force herself to speak above a whisper. "I—I am Adaliah, widow of Itthobaal, and…granddaughter of Leah, wife of Yosef." Maybe Yahweh would remember Grandmother. "My son and I need food, or we will die. Soon. If You are there, will You help us?"

Her whisper fell silent. In the following moments she strained her ears. A breeze rustled the leaves of the olive tree. Somewhere nearby a gull called and was answered by another. No god's voice answered. No olives appeared on the tree, nor potatoes in the desolate garden.

Shoulders slumped in defeat, she returned to the house.

Danel slept much of the day. Adaliah too dozed off and on, though hers was not a restful sleep. Demons marched through her dreams, taunting her. She woke more than once with her heart pounding, her body hot with a guilty certainty that she was at fault for everything. Her mother's death. Itthobaal's death. And now Danel's.

Those last few moments of her husband's life replayed themselves in her mind. Her name shouted from within the burning workshop. His curses. Danel's defenseless body lying on the ground, overcome by smoke, and his choking, gasping attempts to gulp air into his lungs.

*"Worthless wretch."*

The bedchamber seemed to echo with Itthobaal's final words. *"Help me!"* And what had she done? Nothing. She'd stood watching as the burning roof crushed the life out of him. And now the gods were extracting their vengeance by forcing her to stand by and watch her son's life seep away.

She rose from her pallet and stood gazing down at Danel. He looked so small, so frail.

*If you had been born to a different mother, you would be well.*

A few days ago, the thought would have summoned a flood of tears, but Adaliah had none left to shed. She slipped out of the room.

In the living chamber she stood in the middle of the floor. Dazzling rays of afternoon sunlight shone outside the front window but did little to illuminate the room. The few furnishings inside were cast in dreary shadows. She crossed to her worktable and rested a hand on the stool beside it, where Danel liked to sit to watch her prepare their meals. Her fingers trailed across the wooden surface, felt the rough gouges from her knife, and Maresheh's before hers. When she was gone, this would become Tanytha's worktable. She raised her gaze to the shelf. Tanytha's dishes.

The thought brought her neither sorrow nor pleasure. Her soul was numb save for a deep, consuming feeling of regret. How foolish of her, to fight and scratch to keep this pitiful house and its meager furnishings. Why hadn't she accepted Badahur's first offer at once? Or Resheph's? The house she'd placed such value on would soon become their tomb.

The fire beneath her cooking stone had burned down low, and the woodbox was empty. Danel hadn't kept his word to replenish their fuel supply. She glanced at the curtained doorway to the bedchamber. Should she wake him? No. She'd let him sleep. Tonight, she would grind the last of the grain, would cook them each a little cake of bread, and then perhaps they would sit up on the roof for a while, and find pictures in the stars to show each other. He would like that.

Taking the basket Danel used to carry wood, she slipped out of the house. The streets of Zarephath were quiet this evening. She encountered only a handful of people on her way to the town's gate, and they passed her with bowed heads and averted gazes.

The closest olive grove outside the village yielded a few brittle sticks on the ground. When she judged that she had gathered enough to heat the cooking stone, she headed back to town. On her way she glanced up into the branches, hoping to spot a few low-hanging olives, but all the fruit within reach had been picked and she didn't dare get caught climbing to steal the higher ones. The landowner's guard would see her, and then Danel would die alone and frightened.

By the time she headed for home the sun had sunk in the western sky, and its final rays bathed the village in a brilliant orange light. A robed figure approached from the south. She shielded her eyes to see better. A man. Probably someone from town returning from an errand in the plain. Adaliah lowered her head and hurried toward the gate.

"*Shalom aleichem.*"

At the sound of his greeting, she came to a halt. The Hebrew words, *peace be upon you,* spoken in a deep, resonant voice, fell on her ears like a cool breeze on a hot summer day. She looked into a smiling face. How long had it been since anyone smiled at her with such warmth, and without a hint of disdain?

The man increased his pace, his long walking stick digging into the soil with every stride. When he neared, she saw that his disheveled hair and unkempt beard bore streaks of gray, though he moved with the lithe steps of a younger man. The edges of his head covering were tattered, and his robe soiled. Not wealthy, then, and not anyone she recognized. He carried a bedraggled pack slung across one shoulder.

He approached and stopped before her. Adaliah found she could not look away from his eyes, which were as dark as the sky at midnight, and with a lurking intensity that quickened her pulse.

A moment later she tore her gaze from his and uttered the expected response. "Shalom."

Leaning on his stick, he deepened his smile. "My journey across this parched land has been long and tiring. Would you show kindness to a stranger and bring me a drink of water?"

She glanced around the area. Wasn't there anyone else to welcome the traveler to town so she could get home to Danel? But no one else was in sight.

With a nod, she turned away and headed for the gate. She'd drop the wood off at her house, pick up her water jug and a cup, then return.

His voice from behind halted her step. "If I could burden you further, would you bring me some bread for my evening meal?"

A wild laugh threatened to burst out of her mouth, but she swallowed it. She knew from Grandmother that to offer bread to a stranger was a sacred tradition to the Hebrew people, an offer of hospitality. Was that what this man wanted? A meal and a place to rest his head after his journey? If only he knew what he was asking of her.

She turned back to him. "Sir, my grandmother was Hebrew, like you. I know what you ask of me, but..." That direct gaze seemed to pierce her, compelling her to comply. Oh how she wished she could! Would he even believe her if she said as much? Probably not. He would think she was making excuses to be quickly rid of him.

She returned his stare with an unblinking one of her own. "As surely as the Lord your God lives, I have nothing but a handful of grain and a few drops of oil." She extended her basket for his inspection. "I have gathered wood so I can cook this last meal for my son and myself. And after we eat it..." She drew a shuddering breath and squared her shoulders. "We will die."

A dark fire seemed to flicker in his eyes. "Listen to me. Don't be afraid. Go ahead and do as you've said, but first make a small cake for me. For this is what the Lord God of Israel says." His voice took on a fervor that sent blood racing through her veins. "'The grain in your jar will not be used up, and the jug of oil will not run dry until the day the Lord sends rain upon the land.'"

For the span of several shallow breaths she could not move. His words held out a hope so slim, so evasive, that she dared not believe them. But he spoke with a conviction that stirred her soul. Was this Yahweh's answer to the plea of a desperate widow who didn't even believe He existed?

The prophet—for that must be what he was—broke the moment with a smile. "Go. I'll wait here for your return."

Somehow her feet began to move. She hugged the basket of sticks close to her body as she wound her way through the streets, his words circling round and round in her head. *"The grain in your jar will not be used up, and the jug of oil will not run dry."* A thrill of excitement shot through her body, and before she knew it, she was running.

When she burst through the door, she found Danel sitting on his stool, waiting for her. His eyes, dulled from hunger, dropped to the basket.

"I'm sorry, Imma. I should have gone for the wood."

"Never mind that." She rushed over to him, her nerves tingling, and pulled him into a quick hug. Then she thrust the wood into his hands. "Quick. Build up the cook fire while I make the bread."

Interest sparked in his eyes, but he obeyed without questioning her. As he fed sticks into the grate and blew the embers into flame, she took down the grain jar and jug of oil. Her hand trembled as she reached inside the jar and scooped a handful. She fought the instinct to measure out only a small amount. No, the tradition of hospitality and the prophet's promise urged her to be generous. She tilted the jar to fill her hand. Then she dropped to her knees and spread the grain on the quern. Using both hands, she worked her grinding stone. As she crushed the grain beneath the heavy stone, Itthobaal's reprimand from many weeks ago came back to her as if spoken only yesterday. *"After nearly five years I would think you could manage a better cake of bread."* She exerted more effort. There would be no unground pieces in the cake she made for the man of God.

When the flour was as fine as she could make it, she scooped it into a shallow bowl. Then she took the oil jug from its place on the shelf. Her breath caught in her chest, she upended the jug over the bowl. A thin stream of oil dripped onto the flour. She added a pinch of salt for flavor and mixed the dough with her fingers until every grain was incorporated. Then she patted the dough between her palms to form a cake.

"Is the stone hot?" she asked Danel.

He tested the surface with a finger and then nodded.

Though heat wafted from the cooking stone, Adaliah hovered over it, watching the bread cook. Before long it had gone from a pasty lump to a golden-brown mound, as perfectly formed as any she had ever made.

Danel eyed it morosely. "It isn't a very big loaf."

She knew what he was thinking, that they would barely have two bites each.

"This isn't for us." She retrieved a clean cloth from a shelf and wrapped the warm bread in it.

A question appeared on his face, but before he could ask she thrust a cup into his hand and snatched up the water jar.

"Come with me."

They left the house together. A mounting sense of expectation had built in her as she walked, and her steps were hurried. Danel trotted beside her, struggling to keep up, but she slowed only a little. What if she reached the gate and the prophet was gone? What if someone else had offered him hospitality in her absence, someone wealthier? Someone more deserving?

She needn't have worried. The man sat where she'd left him, just outside the village gate. At their approach he got to his feet, pulling himself up with his staff.

He fixed his gaze on Danel. "Shalom to you."

Confusion creased the child's gaunt face. He didn't have the benefit of a Hebrew grandmother, as she did, so he seemed uncertain what to say. He remained silent.

To cover his lack of response, Adaliah extended the warm cloth bundle toward the man of God. He nodded his thanks and unwrapped the cake. She gestured for Danel to hold out the cup, and she filled it with water. As she did, the man tore the loaf in two and lifted both pieces to the sky.

"Thanks be to You, Lord God, for this bread and the faith with which it was prepared."

Danel watched the prayer through eyes as round as a pair of Itthobaal's bowls. With the first bite, a satisfied smile appeared on the prophet's face, and he devoured the rest with obvious enjoyment.

"Yahweh has indeed blessed me through you this day," he told her as he accepted the cup from her hands. "May blessings flow from His throne to fill your house."

"Thank you." She bowed her head to receive his blessing, struggling with a way to remind him of his promise. "Will you honor us by coming to our house?"

Danel shot a quick look at her, and she placed a calming hand on his shoulder.

"We have a room upstairs," she went on. "It is small, but it is yours as long as you like."

She held her breath, afraid he would refuse the offer. If she got home to discover that her grain jar and oil remained empty, he would no doubt be gone when she returned. But if he came with them, perhaps his words would hold true.

The man extended his arms wide, one hand still holding his staff. "I accept."

He followed them through the streets of Zarephath, and they reached the house without encountering anyone. She pushed the door open and then stood back respectfully to allow him to enter.

Before he did, he rested a hand on the doorframe and once again lifted his gaze to the sky. "Lord God, fill this house from the abundance of Your heavenly storehouses."

The look of fascinated curiosity on Danel's face would have made her laugh if her insides weren't tangled into tense knots. She followed him into the house.

The man stood in the center of the living chamber and examined the room with a sweeping gaze. Then he pointed at the stairway out in the courtyard.

"My room is up there?" he asked.

Adaliah nodded, and he started in that direction.

Danel stepped in front of him, forcing him to stop. "I am Danel, and my mother is Adaliah. What is your name?"

Chagrined, Adaliah realized she hadn't even stopped to ask the stranger's name.

"I am Elijah." He looked from Danel to her, a knowing smile hovering at the corners of his lips. "Now I must sleep after my long journey, and your mother will make your evening meal."

With a nod, he climbed the stairs. When his sandaled feet disappeared upstairs, Adaliah flew across the room. She took the jar from the shelf and set it on the worktable. With trembling fingers, she plunged her hand inside—and withdrew a fistful of grain.

The bread she made for Danel and herself that evening was seasoned with her own grateful tears.

# CHAPTER FOURTEEN

Dawn found Adaliah already awake on her pallet. A full belly the night before, and the hope of more, had brought her the first peaceful sleep in many weeks. Though their meal was only bread, it had felt like a feast. But now, in the quiet hours of the morning, fear snaked back into her mind. What if the miracle of the grain and the oil was only for one meal? Would she rise to find the man of God—Elijah, he said—gone and her jar empty once again?

With silent movements, she donned her day tunic and slipped from the bedchamber. She hurried to the worktable but then hesitated. Uncertainty waged a war with belief in her mind as she stared at the grain jar.

"God of Elijah, be merciful."

Her whispered prayer made almost no sound at all in the empty house. She took down the jar, cradled it in one arm, and plunged her other hand in.

Breath left her lungs with a whoosh as her fingers encountered a plentiful amount of grain. She bowed her head, eyes closed, and let the kernels run through her fingers. It was true. Drought might rage through the land, but the Hebrew prophet had chosen her and her son to bless.

A new fear broke in on her thoughts. Months ago, after the last rain fell, word spread throughout the land that a Hebrew prophet was responsible. He had boldly accosted the king of Israel and announced that he had closed up the heavens, and the rains would not fall again until he released them. She glanced upward, to where Elijah slept on Danel's pallet. What if—

No. She shook her head. Yahweh had many prophets, didn't he? Why would *the* prophet journey here, to Zarephath? Prophets were supposed to be wise. Living in this region of Sidon would be neither wise nor safe.

But where had that prophet gone?

Adaliah set the jar down and snatched up her water jug. Water sloshed inside. She emptied it into another jar, of which she had many, thanks to Itthobaal, and left the house.

Women's voices reached her before she arrived at the well. A dozen or so stood in line waiting their turn. Adaliah hadn't been to the well during the daytime in many days, and she swallowed back a fit of nerves as she took her place at the back of the line.

The woman directly in front of her turned, but the greeting died on her lips when she recognized Adaliah. Scorn replaced her smile, and she turned away. She touched the shoulder of the person in front of her to get her attention. That woman too frowned before facing forward. Chatter continued closer to the well, but silence hung heavy at Adaliah's end.

A quick glance told her that Tanytha was not here, for which she spared a grateful thought. This would be difficult enough without her. Adaliah balanced her jug on her shoulder and tried to think of ways to make them talk to her.

Finally, she gathered her courage and spoke in a voice pitched to carry. "I heard there may be rain coming soon."

Of course, she had heard no such thing, but the comment served its purpose. Everyone turned toward her. One or two wore hopeful expressions, but most eyed her with scorn.

"You've lost your mind," said a woman near the front of the line. Adaliah recognized her as Keprea, one of Tanytha's friends. "The sky is as clear as the glass in the royal palace windows."

Guarding her expression, Adaliah nodded. "I feared as much. Just fruitless wishes, I'll wager." She shrugged. "I suppose the prophet who caused this drought isn't ready to end it yet."

Mariet, whose husband owned an olive press, turned to the woman next to her. "I wish Jezebel would find him and put him to the sword, like she did the others. Perhaps killing him would end his curse."

Several around her laughed, but Adaliah's ears pricked.

"The queen would kill a prophet of the Hebrew God?" she asked.

The question drew laughter.

"Not only would she do so, but she has done. Many times," Keprea told her.

A woman in a crimson robe agreed. "I heard she has already put hundreds of those prophets to the sword, and the only one left has disappeared."

"Gone into hiding, no doubt," someone said.

"He is if he knows what's good for him," the red-robed woman answered.

"But why kill all the Hebrew prophets?" Adaliah asked.

"Are you so foolish that you don't know?" Keprea's lips curved with a mocking smirk. "Jezebel is loyal to Baal and is determined to extend the god's territory. Since moving to the backward kingdom of Israel she has built dozens of shrines to our god."

The woman in front of Keprea nodded, and at least she spoke with less disdain. "Israel's prophets forbid the Hebrews to worship any god but theirs, and they have denounced the queen." A touch of fervor crept into her tone. "Israel has always tolerated fanatics who denounce those who don't worship their God."

Keprea laughed. "Now there are a hundred or so fewer of those fanatics, thanks to the queen."

Though Adaliah had heard Itthobaal speak of Queen Jezebel's slaughter of the Hebrew prophets, she pretended she was hearing the news for the first time. "Perhaps the queen has another reason for killing the…fanatics." The word rested uneasily on her tongue. Did she have a crazed zealot living in her house? "Perhaps she is hoping to kill the prophet of the drought and therefore end his curse."

The comment drew looks of contempt.

"Are you truly so dull witted?" Keprea asked. "Of course that's the reason. Why else would she cast her net so widely?"

Swallowing a surge of resentment, Adaliah nodded. "How stupid of me. She wants to catch…" She paused and pretended to think. "What is the prophet's name?"

Keprea rolled her eyes. "How should I know?"

She turned her back, as did the women directly in front and behind her.

But up ahead, Mariet spoke up. "My husband told me the name. It's unusual." She tapped a finger on her lips, thinking. Then she brightened. "I remember. Elijah. The prophet of the drought's name is Elijah."

The woman in front of her moved away from the well, and Mariet stepped forward to take her place. The line shifted forward.

All except Adaliah, whose feet were stuck fast to the ground while her mind reeled.

When she returned home, the prophet was awake and seated on a cushion, his legs crossed and his hands resting on his knees. She hesitated in the doorway with her water jug balanced on her shoulder. He did not speak but watched her with those intense, dark eyes.

Gathering her courage, she entered the house and pulled the door shut behind her. Moving self-consciously, aware that his gaze never left her, she took a cup from the shelf, filled it with water, and then approached to hand it to him. Still silent, he took it from her, but his features softened with a grateful smile. She set the jug in its usual place, casting about for something to say.

"I hope your sleep was restful," she said.

In answer, he merely inclined his head.

"I-if there's anything I can do to make your stay more comfortable…" Her voice trailed off.

He made no response.

Was he always so quiet? She turned away and busied herself by beginning the morning meal. After taking up the grain jar, she dropped to her knees before the quern and scooped out a generous amount. As the kernels flowed through her fingers onto the quern, the reality of the miracle washed over her again and the hair on her arms rose.

"Something has upset you." Elijah's voice cut through her thoughts and made her jump.

Without looking up at him, she spread the grain into a thin layer and picked up the grinding stone. "It's…odd. Having a stranger in the house." She flashed a quick smile before applying herself to her task.

"Perhaps," he said. "But that is not the worry I see in your face."

Eyes averted, she considered how to answer. She hadn't had time to process the knowledge that she was housing the prophet of the drought. What would happen if Tanytha discovered him? Or Fayez? If that happened, a message would be sent to the palace in Israel before the day was out, notifying the king and queen of this man's whereabouts. And what would happen to Danel and her when the queen's soldiers arrived? Would they use their swords on the prophet's friends along with him?

Kernels crushed with a satisfactory crunch beneath her stone, a tangible reminder that she was being rewarded for welcoming Yahweh's prophet into her home. The reward was far more precious than just grain and oil. For herself and her son it was life.

"I talked with some women at the well this morning." He didn't need to know how unusual a conversation with anyone had become in recent days. "The drought continues with no sign that the rains will return soon."

"They will not." He spoke the words flatly, not mere conjecture but a fact.

She kept her eyes lowered, focused on her hands at work. "They say the man who conjured this drought is Hebrew. A prophet."

Her statement met with a low chuckle. "Is that what they say?"

"Yes." She looked up, into his eyes. "And that the prophet's name is Elijah."

The humor on his features deepened. "It seems Ahab has not kept my identity a secret."

Her jaw went slack. "It *is* you."

He splayed his hands. "As you say."

A million questions flooded her mind. "But why? The land is thirsty. Crops are dying, and"—an image of Boz rose before her—"animals are dying. Unless the rains come soon, people too will die for lack of water. We have a deep well here in Zarephath, but what of others? Don't you care that people are suffering?"

Her voice rose with each question until she practically shouted the last one. Snapping her mouth shut, she cast a glance at the curtain behind which Danel slept.

"I care." Elijah bowed his head until his chin rested on his chest. "The Lord my God cares."

"Then send the rain." Her hands fell away from the grinding stone. "They say if you but speak the word, the rains will return."

"That is true." He looked up then, and her heart twisted at the depths of the sorrow in his eyes. "My voice is not my own, but the Lord's. My words have no power on their own, and I have sworn to say nothing except at Yahweh's prompting."

Adaliah slumped backward onto her heels. "Why does your God want people to suffer?"

Pain creased his face. "Yahweh loves His people with a fierce devotion, but after a long line of disobedient kings, they have forgotten Him. They call on lifeless statues to rescue them and deny the One who controls the earth and the seas, the heavens and the rain." Passion crept into his voice, and his eyes blazed. "As the king's heart lies, so do the hearts of the people. King Ahab must rid the land of pagan high places and turn his whole heart to the Lord his God, as King Jehoshaphat of Judah has done, and his father before him. The people must acknowledge Yahweh as the One True God."

A throbbing pain started in her head, and she closed her eyes. He spoke with such fervor that she might be persuaded if she listened long enough. The grain on the quern was proof that Elijah's God had power. More than Baal? Perhaps, since He appeared to have taken command of the god of storm's domain. And at least the Hebrew God cared about widows and orphans, whereas Baal apparently cared for nothing except ensuring a constant flow of blood on his altar. But what difference would the belief of one widow make to a thirsty world? None.

She rubbed her eyes with a thumb and forefinger. All this talk of gods made her weary. "Be that as it may, you won't be of much use to your God if it becomes known that you are here."

He cocked his head, his expression cautious. "How so?"

And the women had laughed at her for her lack of knowledge!

She shook her head. "Don't you know that all the prophets in Israel are dead? Queen Jezebel has put them all to death."

Blood drained from his face, leaving him pale. "All of them?"

He looked so appalled she was moved to pity. "That's what the women said this morning," she told him in a soft voice. "They say you are the only one left."

"I knew." His eyes fluttered closed, and he slapped a fist to his chest. "In here, I knew but I didn't want to believe it." He leaped to his feet and began to pace around the room. "The Lord hid me away to save me."

When he lifted his face toward the ceiling, Adaliah saw a tear slip from his eye and disappear into his hair. His lips moved in a silent prayer.

A soft sigh from the other room told her Danel was beginning to wake. Though she hated to intrude on the man's grief, they must decide what was to be done, and quickly.

She got to her feet and hurried to stand in front of him. "If it becomes known in Zarephath that the prophet Elijah is alive and living in my house, the queen will hear of it in short order.

And then your God will be bereft of any prophet to speak for Him." She gripped his arm. "No one can know."

"Yahweh would not send me here only to die. He will keep guard over me until His purposes are fulfilled." With a visible effort, he composed himself. "But neither does He condone acting foolishly." A struggle took place on his face, and then his expression cleared. "It shall be as you say. To any who ask, I am a Hebrew man looking for employment near the Great Sea."

The story sounded believable.

She nodded her agreement. "Since I have recently fallen upon hard times, no one will question my decision to rent my upper room to a stranger."

He looked disapproving. "In truth I am not renting your room. The Lord my God forbids me to bear false witness."

"But your God sent you here. As you say, He doesn't intend to have you killed within days of arriving. Besides, I am being rewarded in return for sheltering and feeding you." She gestured toward the grain jar. "That is a sort of payment, is it not?"

A conspiratorial smile curved his lips. "I suppose it is."

"What shall we call you?"

His gaze was distant as he considered. "There is a name which means *God is gracious.* And He truly is. I shall be known as Johanan."

He spoke the name on a chuckle, which quickly gained momentum and became a belly laugh.

Adaliah eyed him with caution. From tears of grief to unexplained laughter within a few breaths. Were all prophets subject to such wild emotions?

"Why are you laughing?" she asked.

"One of the pleasures of spending much time in communion with Yahweh is that sometimes He reveals things that are to come." He wiped tears from his eyes. "One day, a long time from now, there will be a man of God named Johanan. In his language the name is pronounced John, and the people will call him Elijah." He shook his head, his chest still heaving with mirth. "My God enjoys a good laugh."

To that, Adaliah had no answer. A God with a sense of humor? Perhaps the prophet was a little mad. As she returned to her grinding stone, she decided she wouldn't leave Danel alone with their guest.

# CHAPTER FIFTEEN

Danel received notice of their guest's name change with suspicion.

He eyed the prophet across the mat while they waited for Adaliah to cook their morning bread. "If your name is Elijah, why must I call you Johanan?"

"It would be best if his real name is a secret." Adaliah flipped a half-cooked cake on the flat rock with the tips of her finger and thumb. "Just between us three."

He turned his head to give her an uncertain look. "Why?"

Before answering she turned the other cakes, her mind working to come up with a reason the child would accept. "Because he likes that name a lot. It means *God is gracious.*"

"What does *gracious* mean?"

She peeked at the underside of the first cake. "It means kind. God is kind."

He considered that. "What does Elijah mean?"

The prophet, who wore an amused smile, answered, "Elijah means *My God is Yahweh.*"

"Yahweh." Danel tried the name as though tasting a new food. "Is that your God's name?"

Elijah nodded. "He has many names, but that's what we call Him."

Confusion settled on Danel's features. "Then Elijah is a good name for you, isn't it?"

The prophet leaned back on his cushion and laughed. "Indeed it is. My father thought so when he gave it to me."

"Then why—"

"Because that's what he wants," Adaliah put in quickly, hoping to put an end to this conversation.

Danel was an intelligent child and had always been curious, but she was losing patience with the questions. It wasn't wise to give a four-year-old too much information and expect him to hold his tongue.

Clearly, Elijah disagreed.

"There are some powerful people who are unhappy with me," he explained to the boy. "If they heard that a man named Elijah lived with you, they would be unhappy with you too."

Irritated, she scowled at the man of God over Danel's head.

"Is it the priests?" Eyes round, Danel lowered his voice to a whisper. "Would they take me away from Imma and offer me to the gods?"

Adaliah caught her breath. She had hoped he hadn't understood Fayez's suggestion that day at the temple, but apparently he grasped more than she realized.

Elijah's features softened. "No, not the priests," he answered, his voice tender. He opened his mouth to continue but then fell silent. His gaze focused on something unseen by anyone except him, and then his lips curved into a slow smile. "Have no fear of the priests and their false gods, little one. One day you too will serve the Only True God."

Wonder crept over Adaliah at the words. Was that a prophecy? Could Elijah's God see her son's future?

In the way of children, Danel accepted the word without question. "Will I have to change my name too?"

The prophet laughed. "I don't know what Yahweh will ask of you, but if He gives you a new name it will be a good one."

The bread was finally cooked, and Adaliah slid three generous cakes onto the platter, glad to interrupt this uncomfortable conversation. She set the tray on the mat and lowered herself to her cushion.

Danel eyed the bountiful meal with awe. "The loaves are big today."

"We have *Johanan* to thank," she told him, emphasizing the name.

Elijah shook his head. "We must thank the One who provides for all our needs."

He leaned forward and took up a browned cake. With a slow, deliberate movement he tore the loaf into two pieces, then lifted them both in the air.

"*Baruch atah, Adonai Eloheinu, Melech haolam, haMotzi lechem min haaretz.*"

When he lowered his hands, Danel asked, "What did you say?"

Elijah set half of the bread on the platter. "It means, *Blessed are You, Infinite One, who brings forth bread from the earth.*"

A frown appeared on his face as he looked at the meal platter. He glanced around the room, his gaze settling on Adaliah's worktable. Then he turned a look of compassion on her. She flushed and lowered her head. He must be accustomed to more than just bread to break his nightly fast. Did he only now realize how impoverished was this house to which his God had sent him?

"Might we have a bit of oil to dip the bread in?" he asked.

She opened her mouth to refuse because they had to conserve their supply. But then she saw the twinkle in his eyes. If his word was true—and she was beginning to believe it was—they would have oil enough to last until the rains came. More relaxed than she had been in months, she rose to do the man of God's bidding.

After a few days of bread morning and evening, Adaliah's heart rejoiced to see Danel's face regain some of its roundness. The dark splotches beneath his eyes faded, and he resumed his daily chore of gathering wood for their cooking fire. He moved with more vigor than she had seen since Itthobaal's death.

He was clearly fascinated with the man of God. Elijah spent much of the day upstairs in his room, either sleeping or praying or doing whatever it was that prophets did. But during mealtimes, the three sat around the mat and Elijah told them stories of Yahweh and the children of Israel. Some of the tales were familiar to Adaliah, like the very first man and woman, who were formed by Yahweh's own hands, and the beautiful garden in which they lived. Others she had not heard, such as the boy who faced down a giant while a whole army of soldiers stood watching and terrified. She listened as eagerly as Danel while Elijah described a bush that glowed with the fire of God but did not burn, and how Yahweh sent bread from heaven to feed his people while they wandered in the wilderness. She had a vague memory of that story, but now it lingered in her mind with new significance. Bread from heaven. Apparently, Yahweh placed a great value on bread.

She said as much one evening several days after the prophet's arrival as they sat down to their meal.

"Oh yes," he told her solemnly. "Bread is nearly as old as mankind. The first man ate bread after he was shut out of Yahweh's garden. When our father Abraham was returning home after defeating four kings he was welcomed with bread, and afterward he offered bread to three angels who came to his tent."

"What are angels?" Danel asked.

The man of God never seemed to grow tired of the child's questions. Indeed, he answered each one with a patience Adaliah didn't possess herself.

"Angels are heavenly beings created by the Lord God to serve Him, and to act as His messengers." He tore off a piece of bread and dipped it into the bowl of salted oil on the platter. "They're very powerful, and most people never see them."

"Have you ever seen angels?"

"Yes, little one. Yahweh has been gracious to me and has allowed me to see many things."

The child's eyes shone. "I would like to see an angel."

Elijah laughed. "Perhaps one day the Lord God will show you one."

Adaliah studied the loaf in her hand. Morning and evening she was filled with awe when she measured out grain for their bread. The jar was never full, but neither was it ever empty. The same with the jug, which provided her with a constant supply of oil.

"Yahweh doesn't only use angels to do His bidding," Elijah told Danel. "He is the Lord of all living things. Animals. Fish. Birds." He grinned. "Before I came here the Lord God sent ravens to me every day, bringing bread and meat."

Now it was Adaliah's turn to stare at him, dumbfounded. "Ravens brought your meals?"

Eyes twinkling, he nodded. "Every morning and every evening."

"But where did it come from?"

Chewing, he shrugged.

"I think somebody cooked it, like Imma," Danel said with the certainty of a child who has figured out a puzzle. "Then she gave it to the birds and told them to take it to you."

"Perhaps." Elijah cocked his head, considering. Then his expression cleared. "I did not question Yahweh's provision. I merely received and gave thanks."

Very privately Adaliah thought a little meat would be welcome. If Elijah's God had supplied him with meat before, would He do it again? But she didn't want to appear ungrateful for the miracle of grain and oil, so she kept the thought to herself.

The door opened without warning, and Tanytha strode into the room. She stopped and stared at the three of them.

Surprise showed clearly on her features, and not a pleasant surprise.

"What are you doing?" The question shot across the room like an arrow.

Elijah's eyebrows arched, but he remained silent.

"We are having a meal." Adaliah gestured to the platter, where half of her bread waited. "Would you like to join us?"

The woman's mouth snapped shut. Her gaze fixed on Elijah, and her eyes narrowed. "Who is this?"

Her tone held such an accusation that Adaliah flushed at the blatant rudeness. The reason wasn't hard to discern. She'd come expecting to find them starving or even dead, and she wasn't pleased to discover them in good health and enjoying a meal.

Adaliah started to answer, but Elijah stopped her with a glance. He rose in one smooth movement and crossed to stand before Tanytha, his expression cordial.

"I am called Johanan."

Adaliah hid a smile at the careful wording.

Elijah dipped his head in greeting and continued. "I've recently come to town, and this woman has been kind enough to offer me hospitality."

Tanytha's gaze stabbed Adaliah. "You've taken in a boarder?"

Adaliah returned the glare without blinking, her face impassive. "Since I have been denied the ability to earn a living, it seemed a good solution." She gestured toward the stairway. "We do have the room."

A purple flush crept over Tanytha's face, and she clenched her hands into fists. "I would like to speak to you." Her glower slid from Adaliah to Elijah. "Outside."

She whirled and strode out of the house without waiting for an answer.

With difficulty Adaliah maintained a serene demeanor as she rose from her cushion. She smiled at Danel, who had watched the encounter closely but silently. Elijah was staring after Tanytha, his expression thoughtful.

Outside, Tanytha waited for her with blazing eyes. "You don't fool me," she hissed.

Adaliah shook her head. "What do you mean?"

"That man." Tanytha stabbed a finger at the house. "He's not a boarder. He's your lover."

Stunned, Adaliah could only stare at her.

"Your husband not dead two months and already you've taken another man into your bed, and with your son in the same house." Disgust curled her lips. "You're nothing but a common harlot."

Anger, hot and sudden, flooded Adaliah. She stepped forward and thrust her face close to Tanytha's. "I have made an honorable arrangement, one by which I can feed my son. I am left with no other choice, thanks to you. But you've done all the harm you can. There's nothing else you can do to us."

She had the satisfaction of seeing the woman's eyes widen. Clearly Tanytha had expected to confront a lamb and had found a bear instead.

For a long moment they stood, toe to toe. Then Tanytha's eyes narrowed to slits, and her lips twisted with distain. She glanced at the house and then turned and stomped away.

Alone, Adaliah's rage dissolved like vapor. In truth, Tanytha could still do them a great deal of harm. If she spread her vicious rumor, Adaliah would become even more of a pariah than she already was. And if Tanytha discovered Elijah's true identity, their lives would be in grave peril.

# CHAPTER SIXTEEN

The following morning Elijah announced over their morning meal that he would accompany Danel on his wood-gathering chore. Though clearly pleased to have company, Danel once again answered the statement with a question.

"Why?"

"Because I would like to gather twice as much as usual. Tomorrow I will celebrate Shabbat." Elijah picked up his cup. "It is a day of rest for my people. We do no work on Shabbat, and I would be pleased if you would honor the day with me." He eyed Adaliah over the rim of his cup. "Both of you."

"Shabbat," Danel repeated slowly. "What will we do on Shabbat?"

"Nothing," Adaliah answered. "My grandmother sometimes observed Shabbat, after my grandfather rested with his ancestors."

Elijah's eyebrow rose. "Only after his death?"

She shrugged. "My grandfather was Sidonese, not Hebrew. Grandmother didn't return to the ways of her childhood until he was gone. Some days she would not leave her bedchamber at all, and she told me she was celebrating Shabbat."

"We will sit around all day and do nothing?" Danel's expression told them he didn't relish the idea of an entire day of inactivity.

"Not at all." Elijah dabbed his last piece of bread in the oil. "Shabbat is more than a day of rest. It's a day of joyful remembrance. The Lord God instructed His people to *remember* and to *observe*. So, we remember that the Lord made the heavens and the earth in six days, and we observe the seventh day, when God rested from His labors. We rest from ours, and we celebrate our lives and Yahweh's blessings." He looked at Adaliah. "Many Hebrew people who live in foreign lands recall the Lord God's commandments but not the reasons for them."

Though it was entirely possible that Grandmother had forgotten many things, the conversation didn't sit well with Adaliah. A day of rest wasn't bad in itself, and indeed would be welcome. But they were not Hebrew. Elijah had introduced the Hebrew custom of thanking his God before every meal, and that was right since their food came directly from Yahweh's hand. But was this Shabbat observation one more step toward turning her home into a Hebrew household? She did not want her son to become a fanatic, like the many Israeli prophets that Jezebel had put to the sword. Serving Elijah's God did not bode well for a long life these days.

"My mother used to grow angry with Grandmother on those days, saying she was making more work for others while she lazed about on her pallet." Adaliah rose from her cushion and gathered up the empty dishes. "If the women of the household refused to work one day in every week, the men's bellies would protest."

Elijah did not seem offended. "Faithful Hebrew women, like Hebrew men, have learned to complete their work before sundown when Shabbat begins. Even in the wilderness when

Yahweh fed His children with bread from heaven, He sent twice as much on the sixth day so they would not have to gather on the seventh."

"So the women work twice as hard preparing for this day of rest?" Her face heated as she spoke, and she avoided the prophet's eye. "No wonder they fall exhausted onto their pallets and sleep all the next day."

"Shabbat is a day of plenty," Elijah told her. "A day of spiritual enrichment, and even meals are enjoyed in a more elaborate way than any other day. It is a joyful time."

"Elaborate meals?" Though she tried to keep the scorn from her laugh, she saw in Danel's surprised expression that she failed. Her face burned hotter. "That would be a welcome change."

She turned her back on them and rested her hands on the worktable as shame washed over her. How ungrateful she sounded. Elijah's God was feeding them with bread from heaven just as He had done for His people in the wilderness, and all she could think of was how she wanted more. She sounded like Tanytha.

A tendril of fear wormed into her thoughts. If she wasn't properly grateful, would Elijah's God stop filling her grain and oil jars?

Swallowing her pride, she turned toward Elijah again. "I'm sorry. I am truly thankful for Yahweh's gifts. If your God wants us to observe Shabbat, we will."

Instead of the anger she expected to find in his face, she looked into eyes full of compassion.

"The Lord God's gifts are not conditional," he told her softly. "He did not choose to bless you as a reward for anything you have done or promised to do. Being thankful is enough." His gaze shifted to Danel, and he spoke in a lighter tone. "But I would still like to help you gather wood today. And one other thing."

The boy perked up. "What?"

"I would like to meet other Hebrews, if there are any living here." He turned an inquisitive look on Adaliah.

She knew of several Hebrew families in Zarephath, but she didn't think Elijah would enjoy meeting them. Not one adhered to the commands of Yahweh. Like King Ahab, they acknowledged Yahweh but also worshipped the gods, particularly Baal and Asherah.

A thought occurred to her. "There is one man. I met him some months ago." She described the boatbuilder who had helped her the day she tumbled down the steep path. "I don't know his name," she finished. "Only that he spoke to me in Hebrew and treated me kindly."

"Then our day is planned," Elijah told Danel. He raised an eyebrow in her direction. "If your mother agrees to let you act as my guide to the harbor."

Adaliah hesitated only a moment. In the days since the prophet arrived, she'd dismissed the idea that he was mad. Devoted? Yes. Even fanatical about his God. But Danel would be safe with him, of that she was certain.

She gave her approval with a nod.

"Imma!" Danel burst through the door that afternoon with a shout.

Adaliah lifted her gaze from the torn tunic she was mending, and her heart lightened at the look of excitement on her son's face. When had she last seen him this enthusiastic about anything? Long before the tragedy that took his father's life.

"We've been to the sea, and we helped a man build a boat."

Elijah entered at a more sedate place, but his expression held no less pleasure than the child's.

"You found the boatbuilder, then?" she asked.

"We did," the prophet said. "His name is Shemen son of Nebat, and his family is from Kinneret in Israel."

"He's building a big boat on the beach," Danel told her, his voice animated. "A man paid him money to do it. And Elijah is—"

"Johanan," she corrected quickly.

The child rolled his eyes. "*Johanan* is going to help him build it, and he said I could help sometimes, and maybe he will even pay me."

She couldn't help but catch a bit of his excitement. "Really? And what will you do with your money?"

He answered without a moment's hesitation. "I will buy apples and share them with you and Eli—Johanan."

A bittersweet pang shot through her heart. Her son had not yet seen his fifth year and already he knew the ravages of poverty and hunger. Yet he still thought of others.

She dropped her mending and pulled him into a hug. "That is a very good plan."

He allowed himself to be hugged briefly and then pulled away. "And Shemen sent something for you." Turning to the prophet, he said, "Are you going to give it to her?"

From behind his back Elijah produced a bundle of oiled fabric, which he extended to her. "Shemen ben Nabat sends greetings and his wishes that you enjoy an abundant Shabbat meal."

Numbly, Adaliah got to her feet. When her fingers touched the parcel, she felt the shape of a fish and something else wrapped in the cloth. Crossing to her worktable, she unfolded the bundle to find not only a fat fish but also an onion and three small potatoes. Tears filled her eyes. This gift was no less a miracle than Yahweh's grain and oil.

Dashing away the tears, she rewrapped the cloth and then turned. "I will prepare our Shabbat meal before sundown," she told them. "Then tomorrow we can all remember and observe."

"Then Esau forgave Jacob for deceiving him," Elijah told Danel. "And they parted in peace."

They had finished their abundant meal, and it had truly been a joyful feast. After a diet of only bread for nearly a week, and very little before that, Adaliah felt almost sinful eating her fill. But Elijah had kept up a constant dialogue, regaling them with tales from the Hebrew people's history.

She glanced at the remnants of their meal, which she had covered so they could eat again in the evening. Sitting on her cushion and listening to Elijah's stories was far more enjoyable than she expected, though her fingers did itch to pick up her mending and make use of the time in some productive way. Observing a full day of rest would take some getting used to.

Danel wore a puzzled expression as he listened to the end of the story. "Why did Jacob steal from his brother?" he asked.

"Perhaps he was jealous of his father's affections," the prophet replied.

The child considered this, and then nodded slowly. "Like Tanytha is jealous because Abba loved me."

Adaliah's mouth gaped open. Danel had never voiced such a thought to her, so she had assumed he didn't know the reason for Tanytha's harsh words and vicious looks. She should have known better, since he was such a perceptive child.

"Jealousy is one of the oldest sins, and perhaps the most powerful," Elijah told the boy, his tone solemn. "It causes men to hate, to steal, and even to kill."

Danel looked so disturbed at the words that she opened her mouth to assure him that Tanytha wouldn't kill him. Then she closed it again, the protest unspoken. Hadn't his half sister tried to do exactly that by poisoning the entire village against them to arrange their deaths by starvation?

"There were once two brothers," Elijah said, beginning another story. "The elder was named Cain, and the younger

Abel. Abel offered an excellent gift to the Lord, and Yahweh looked on his gift with favor. But Cain's gift wasn't from his heart, as his brother's was, and Yahweh sees into men's hearts. Because of that, He wasn't pleased with Cain's gift. Cain grew jealous of the Lord's favor, and he killed Abel."

Adaliah closed her eyes, the horror of brother killing brother washing over her. This was another story Grandmother hadn't told her.

"What happened to Cain?" Danel asked, completely entranced.

"The Lord cursed him and sent him far away from his home as punishment." The prophet's voice took on a note of sadness. "That was the first time any man killed another, though it was not the last. Yahweh created people out of His great love, and His desire is for us to love each other. To cause the death of another person is an act that He cannot allow to go unpunished."

Adaliah's heart stuttered to a halt in her chest. Guilt crushed in on her, so strong the peace of this Shabbat shattered like a broken bowl. She had caused the death of not one, but two people. Would Yahweh one day curse and punish her?

# CHAPTER SEVENTEEN

Adaliah rose well before dawn and took her water jug to the well. Days had passed since Tanytha's last visit and her absurd accusation. Had she spread her latest poison throughout the town? Though Adaliah's instinct was to take refuge in her house with her unending supply of grain and oil, the danger of her position lay heavy on her thoughts. She was housing the prophet of the drought. The slightest suspicion about Elijah's identity could endanger Danel and her.

Few women were at the well so early. She counted only five waiting their turn at the bucket, speaking in hushed voices so as not to disturb those sleeping in nearby houses. Relieved, she shouldered her jug and took her place at the end of the line.

The pair directly in front of her turned at her approach. When they recognized her, their expressions changed. She'd grown accustomed to being received with contempt, but did she detect a new tenor to their frowns? Her heart sank. Tanytha's sharp tongue had not been idle.

The woman at the front of the line poured water from the bucket into her jug and turned. Adaliah recognized her as Badahur's first wife, Idra. She passed the bucket with a smile that grew brittle when she caught sight of Adaliah. She left her water jug on the ground and approached with a measured step.

"I hear you've taken up a new line of work." The words dripped scorn.

Adaliah straightened her spine and looked the woman in the eye. "That is true. I've become something of an innkeeper, by taking in a boarder."

"Is that what you're calling him?"

The woman's lip curled, and she included the others in the conversation with a disdainful glance. Their snickers found their mark, and Adaliah flushed.

"I'm able to feed my son thanks to Johanan." She was pleased that her voice held none of the turmoil she felt. "I had no choice but to open my house to a stranger, since no one else saw fit to help us."

Idra folded her arms across her ample bosom. "That may be, but first you tried to worm your way into my house by seducing my husband."

Adaliah gasped. "I don't know what you're talking about."

"She came to Badahur's workshop," Idra told the women, who listened with obvious delight. "She asked him to take her as his wife, and when he refused, she begged him. My son heard her with his own ears."

The young man was at the potter's wheel that terrible day when Adaliah learned of Father's death. She fought a stab of grief at the memory.

"I was accepting his proposal." She looked around the watching faces, silently begging them to believe her. "He asked me to become his wife after I refused to sell him my kiln."

Idra snorted her disbelief. "He has four kilns already. Why would he want another?"

"He—he said…"

The explanation died in the face of the skepticism she saw on every person watching her. There was nothing she could say to convince them. They wanted to believe the worst of her, and they did. Her shoulders slumped.

"Believe what you will." She held her head high, though tears stung her eyes. "Johanan is a boarder in my home, and nothing else. He is a good man, a kind man, and devoted to his Hebrew God."

She could have said more, but she could no longer hold back her tears and she refused to let them fall in front of these uncaring woman. Holding her jug close to her body with both hands, she turned and left the well.

Let them say what they would of her. If they thought her a woman of loose morals, so be it. At least if their tongues were busy talking about her, they wouldn't have time to wonder about Elijah.

Adaliah held her scarf in place beneath her chin as she picked her way down the narrow trail to the beach. The wind held a chill today and whipped the waves into frothy mountains. There were no boats at the harbor this afternoon. Her gaze lingered on the shelf-like cleaning table where a fisherman had refused her coin. That day seemed like years ago, though in reality it had been only a few weeks. Her situation was no longer desperate, her son no longer reduced to stealing fish heads to fill his belly. Thanks to Elijah's God and his friendship with Shemen, their meal tray had not gone empty.

Which was the reason for her errand. At the bottom of the trail she turned right, heading toward the smaller north harbor. Shielding her eyes with a hand, she scoured the shoreline until she found what she was looking for. There, just beyond the promontory, lay the skeleton of a boat and nearby, a tent. Three figures worked there, two men and one beloved boy. She quickened her pace.

Danel caught sight of her as she neared.

"Imma!" With careful movements he set the pouch he held on the ground and raced to greet her. "Did you come to see our boat?"

"I did." She smiled into his eager face and then looked up at the men who had stopped their work. "And to meet the boatbuilder."

Shemen tossed a mallet onto the ground and approached. "But we've met before."

"We have," she agreed, "though I didn't know your name until Johanan told me."

She included Elijah in the conversation with a glance at him. His eyes twinkled with the smile he always wore when she referred to him by his assumed name.

She turned back to Shemen. "I've come to thank you for your kindness and to invite you to share our Shabbat meal tomorrow."

Nearly every day Elijah and Danel returned from their work on Shemen's boat with a gift of food. A few potatoes, carrots, the occasional fish—all added to the bread made from Yahweh's grain and oil to turn their meals into near feasts. She was certain the people in the marketplace had no idea that the Hebrew boatbuilder who bought their wares was supplying the outcast widow they continued to reject. That was one reason she had kept her distance so long. If the villagers discovered her benefactor, the stain of her reputation might besmirch him as well.

But she couldn't continue to accept his gifts without a proper show of gratitude.

Danel rounded on Shemen with a grin. "Yes! You can listen to the stories too." He glanced at Elijah. "My favorite is the one about the boy who killed a giant and then he became the king."

"I am honored by the invitation." Shemen lifted his head to look toward the city. "But my tent is more than two thousand cubits from the town."

"It isn't far," Danel told him. "Johanan and I walk here every day."

He smiled at the boy. "Yes, but I cannot walk that far on Shabbat."

"It is a day of rest," Elijah reminded them. "Therefore we are to limit our travels outside the gates of whatever city we find ourselves in on that special day." He met Adaliah's eye, his eyebrows arched with a question. "There is space for two pallets in my room. And the room next to it is nearly empty."

Inside, she cringed. What would the women of Zarephath say if they discovered that she had *two* men in her house? On the other hand, she could not control what people said of her. Nor did she care. Well, not much.

She smiled at Shemen. "You are welcome to stay the night in our home and celebrate Shabbat with us."

When he accepted, she left them to continue their work.

That Shabbat, their third since Elijah's arrival, was truly a joyful celebration. Shemen arrived well before sundown with a treat from his personal supplies, brought from his recent trip to Sidon—dried apples. Danel danced with glee as Adaliah prepared them for their Shabbat meal.

When the meal had been eaten and the remains covered, they took their cushions out to the courtyard and sat beneath the olive tree, enjoying a salt-scented breeze and more of Elijah's stories from the children of Israel's history. He seemed to have an endless supply, each one designed to highlight an aspect of his God.

"How do you know so much about the past?" Adaliah asked when he finished telling about David's battle with a lion who tried to carry off a sheep from the flock he was tending.

"I learned from my father, who learned from his father before him." The prophet spread his arms to include them all. "This is how we celebrated every Shabbat I can remember."

"It is the same with my family," Shemen told them. "My father and my grandfather took it in turns to tell one tale after another."

Adaliah smiled. "Since we have no grandfathers here, it's your turn."

"Yes." Danel nodded eagerly. "What is your favorite story?"

"That would be the story of Babel," Shemen told the boy. "Have you heard it?"

Danel shook his head, and Shemen leaned back against the tree trunk and began.

"Sometime after the Great Flood—"

"We heard about that," Danel interrupted. "About the huge boat and all the animals and the rain that washed everything away."

"That's the one." Shemen grinned at the boy. "The Lord God told them to multiply and spread out across the earth, but they did not. They had many children, and those children had children, but instead of moving away they all stayed in one place. Sometime later they learned how to make bricks. Together they decided to build a huge city, and in the center of it they built a tower. The tallest tower that was ever made. It stretched way up into the sky"—he lifted his arm above his head, his fingers stretched as far as he could reach—"and still they kept building. Up into the clouds. They wanted to go all the way up to heaven, you see."

Yet another story that Adaliah had not heard from her grandmother. She tried to picture a tower reaching up to the heavens but failed.

"Did they want to climb up to see Yahweh?" Danel asked.

Shemen shook his head. "No. They wanted to make a name for themselves. They thought if they could do something no one had ever done before, they would be important. But the Lord knew what they were doing. He came down and inspected the city, and especially the tower. And He did not like it."

Creases appeared on the boy's brow, and he asked his favorite question. "Why?"

"Because He did not want them to think they could do such magnificent things on their own without Him. Else they might begin to think they did not need Him, as people before the Flood thought. That thinking always leads to evil, something He did not want. Besides, He was not happy that they had disobeyed His instructions to spread out over the earth, so He put a stop to their plans."

Caught up in the story, Adaliah asked a question of her own. "Did your God tear down the tower?"

A smile appeared on Elijah's face.

"No," Shemen told her, grinning. "He did something even better. He created languages."

"Why is that better?" Danel asked.

"Because suddenly the people could not understand each other. One minute they were talking together." Shemen got to his feet and began a pantomime. He turned to one side and plastered on an arrogant expression. "Please pass me a brick so I may add another step to our beautiful tower." Then he whipped around, as though facing the man who'd just spoken and answered in a different voice. "Here is your brick, my friend. Let me fetch the tar for you as well."

He pretended to hand over an invisible brick with a dramatic flourish that made them all laugh.

"But then, all of a sudden, they each spoke in a different language." Shemen resumed his first stance and pretended to accept the brick. "*Babbru meekash potooe.*" Then he leaped into the second man's place. His expression became a comical mask of confusion. "*Kelup probash? Goobey borga bloogah.*"

When the nonsense blather rolled off Shemen's tongue, his audience burst into laughter. Danel collapsed onto his side, shrieking with mirth. Adaliah laughed so hard her sides hurt, and Elijah used the hem of his robe to wipe tears from his face.

Clearly pleased with their reaction, Shemen dropped back into a sitting position on his cushion. "And that's why it was my favorite story as a boy. My father and grandfather each assumed a role and hearing those two babble at each other never failed to amuse us."

"Are you throwing a party now, and your husband only three months gone?"

The sharp voice sliced into Adaliah's thoughts, and her laughter died. Tanytha stood in the doorway, her arms folded across her chest and a glower darkening her features.

Danel fell instantly silent in a way that tore at Adaliah's heart. Shemen cast a confused look at her. Apparently, he had not yet met her stepdaughter or been the subject of her scorn.

Elijah recovered himself first and stood. "Our friend here was entertaining us with a tale. Will you join us?" He extended a hand to indicate she could take his cushion.

Tanytha's eyes narrowed, and for a moment she looked uncertain. Then she recovered.

She ignored the offer and instead spoke to Adaliah. "I need to speak with you."

Without waiting for an answer, she disappeared into the house.

Adaliah excused herself without meeting anyone's eye and hurried after her.

"Where did you get this?" Tanytha demanded as soon as she entered.

The remains of their meal had been uncovered. Tanytha stabbed a finger toward the leftover fish, apples, and bread.

She forced a brittle smile. "My guests are generous."

"No one has seen you for days," Tanytha continued in an accusing tone. "I came here to see if you had come to your senses and moved away."

"Have you not heard?" Adaliah answered as evenly as she could. "My father is dead. I have nowhere to go. Besides"—she allowed a touch of firmness to creep into her tone—"this is our home."

Tanytha's lips pressed into a hard line. "It was my home first."

She looked so much like a pouty child that an unwelcome compassion crept over Adaliah. If what Resheph told her was true, Tanytha was not happy living in her mother-in-law's home. The new infant had no doubt arrived by now, and it must be torture to watch her sister-in-law cuddle a baby while her own arms remained empty. No wonder she kept returning here, to the place where she lived happily with her mother and father.

*What do I care? Tanytha's happiness is not my concern.*

But suddenly the shrewish expression that rested so often on Tanytha's features looked more miserable than hateful.

"Yes, it was," she replied, her voice soft.

Tanytha's eyes widened at the change in tone. She opened her mouth to say something, but apparently thought better of it. Instead, she whirled and headed for the door.

"Wait."

She halted but did not turn.

Unwilling to let the moment end, Adaliah cast about for something to say, or for some gesture of kindness that might show that she would still welcome a relationship between them. Her gaze fell on a cake of bread, and she snatched it up. Hurrying to her table she took one of Itthobaal's beautiful bowls and placed the bread inside.

"Here." She pressed the bowl into Tanytha's hands. "You should have something of Itthobaal's for your own." *And something from me as well.* But she did not mention the gift of bread.

Tanytha's harsh expression remained, but her hands clutched the bowl to her chest as she left.

# CHAPTER EIGHTEEN

Even with Tanytha's unpleasant interruption, the Shabbat celebration was one of the most enjoyable days Adaliah could remember. Not since Danel was a chubby baby had she seen him laugh as he did at Shemen's portrayal of the men at the tower of Babel. When the sun set and the boatbuilder prepared to return to his tent, she invited him to come back the following week, and indeed every Shabbat.

"A gracious invitation," he replied with a princely bow. "I accept."

The days that followed flowed in pleasant succession. Adaliah fetched her water from the well late at night, after Elijah and Danel retired to their pallets, and grew to enjoy the solitude of the task.

The next time Tanytha returned, Adaliah was kneeling before the quern, applying the grinding stone to the day's supply of Yahweh's grain. She burst through the door, as always, and then stopped in the center of the room to stare.

Fighting a surge of irritation, Adaliah fixed a pleasant expression on her face. "Good morning."

"You're grinding grain."

Adaliah shoved the stone forward on the quern. "Indeed."

"Grain is in short supply because of this cursed drought." She came closer, her step slow, and watched Adaliah's motions closely. "The sellers in the market have marked up their prices so high only the rich can afford it."

Adaliah chose to ignore the implied question. She continued her work without answering.

Tanytha took another step. "Your jar was empty when I was last here."

The unmistakable tone of suspicion lay heavy in the statement. A tingle of alarm began in Adaliah's mind. Everything in her told her to guard the secret of the miracle, and yet Elijah's God demanded truthfulness. If she spoke falsely, would the miracle of the grain and oil cease?

She chose a vague response. "And yet we have grain today."

"Where did it come from?" Tanytha demanded in a flat tone.

Adaliah sat back on her heels and looked up at her stepdaughter. "My boarder, Johanan, said it was a gift from his God."

Her head was beginning to ache from trying to come up with obscure answers that would satisfy Tanytha and yet not quite be lies.

"He didn't buy it in the marketplace." A sarcastic laugh blasted from Tanytha's lips. "Does his God have a storehouse somewhere nearby?"

Adaliah heaved an irritated breath. "I don't ask where the grain comes from. All I know is since Johanan came to stay with us, we have had bread every day. That is how I am paid for his room."

There. Let her believe that Elijah had a stash of grain somewhere from which he provided for their needs.

"Who is this Hebrew?" Tanytha's eyes widened with a thought. "Is he one of their prophets?"

Though her nerves tightened into knots at the shrewd guess, Adaliah forced herself not to react. To hide her trembling fingers, she picked up the grinding stone and tackled the grain with force.

"What would a prophet be doing here, in Zarephath?" She let a touch of derision seep into her laugh. "If there are any Hebrew prophets who have escaped Queen Jezebel's soldiers, they are no doubt as far from Sidon as they can get."

Tanytha didn't appear convinced but watched her through slitted eyes.

Adaliah kept working, her gaze fixed on her hands. "Johanan is a devout Hebrew whose family worships their Hebrew God. He became disillusioned when the queen erected temples to Baal across Israel, and he left."

"Someone should tell Fayez," Tanytha said.

Though inside her heart quivered at the mention of the chief priest, Adaliah shrugged. "Tell him what? Worshipping the Hebrew God is not a crime. Besides"—she halted her work long enough to point to the fine flour beneath her stone—"why would I question the gift of grain that feeds us?"

She endured a long, searching look, which she returned without looking away. Then Tanytha snorted and, with another glance at the grain, left the house.

The tension seeped from Adaliah's muscles, and her arms dropped limply to her lap. Did Tanytha believe her story of Elijah's past? She'd never taken Adaliah's word for anything before. And if she didn't this time, the next visitor to her house might be Fayez, or even one of Jezebel's soldiers.

One other disturbing thought niggled at her conscience. Though she had not spoken an outright lie, the story had rolled easily off her tongue. Did Elijah's God hate vague deception as much as He hated outright lies?

That night after sundown, Adaliah lit the lamp and then sat beside Danel in the courtyard to show him how to trace *alep* in a thin layer of coarse sand taken from the beach. She handed the stick to Danel. "Now you try it."

Watching him, she was sharply reminded of her own first efforts to replicate Father's letters. Only, she had used a stylus and a tablet lined with soft clay. A shame Itthobaal's tablets had been burned, and she had no money to buy more. But no matter. Sand smoothed out on a platter served the purpose, and cost nothing.

"Shemen asked about the circumstances of your husband's death," Elijah said.

She looked up to find the prophet sitting on the bottom step of the stairway leading to the roof and upper rooms, watching them.

"I told him about the fire," Danel said in a subdued voice.

Her heart hurt for her son, and she grasped about for something comforting to say. She might be happier without her tyrant husband, but Danel missed his abba. "It was a terrible day."

After a pause, Elijah continued. "Shemen showed quite an interest when Danel told him that his abba was the best potter in all of Zarephath." He cast an amused glance at the child. "He wanted to know if any plans have been made for the kiln."

It seemed everyone wanted to know the fate of her kiln.

"That isn't the first time I've been asked." Something occurred to her, and she looked up. "Is his interest personal? Is the boatbuilder also a potter?"

"No, but he knows one." Danel answered without looking up from a row of perfect aleps.

Elijah explained. "Shemen's brother married the granddaughter of a potter. She learned the trade as a child."

"A woman potter?"

The idea almost made her laugh but only for a moment. Why should a woman not work at the pottery trade? After all, in a village renowned for its kilns, the best one was owned by a woman.

"She is not a potter now. When her grandfather went to be with his ancestors, his work passed into the hands of a cousin."

His tone hinted at something held back. Where was the prophet going with this conversation? From the close way he was watching her, she knew he was about to make a proposal. And what else could it be, since he was telling the owner of a kiln about a potter without a kiln?

"But she would like to work at a potter's wheel again?"

A small smile appeared on Elijah's lips. "She would very much like to. Her grandfather made her a gift on his death-bed—a potter's wheel of her own. If only she had a workshop and a kiln."

Adaliah tore her gaze from his and focused instead on the sand. "You've done well," she told Danel. "Now try this one." She traced *bet* with her finger. "Where do Shemen's brother and his potter wife live?"

"In Kinneret, on the shores of the Sea of Galilee."

"That's where Shemen is from," Danel told her. "His brother builds boats too."

"Does he?" She corrected an errant line in his work and looked up at Elijah. "Is there a request at the end of this conversation?"

He dipped his forehead. "Shemen has received orders for two more boats. Apparently, the drought has stirred an interest in fishing," he added in a dry tone. "His brother is agreeable to joining him here but does not want to leave his wife behind because she is expecting their first child."

Not only a woman potter, but one with child. *Imagine the reaction of Badahur and the other potters of Zarephath.* The idea stirred up a chuckle within Adaliah. But then she sobered.

"I will not sell my kiln," she told Elijah flatly. "One day it will be Danel's."

The child looked up from his work. "My abba said so."

Something in his tone made her look more closely at him. Was that resignation she detected? Didn't he want to grow up and continue his abba's work? She dismissed the question. What did a boy of four know of business and the importance of mastering a trade?

"No one suggested buying the kiln," Elijah said. "From what I understood, Shemen's family is of modest means. No doubt they don't have the money to buy anything. But if they were to come here, she may be able to make use of the kiln. Perhaps an arrangement could be made whereby the profits are shared."

An intriguing idea, she had to admit. An outcast widow and a pregnant female potter launching into business together? The entire village would be outraged—Badahur especially. That thought right there made the idea worth considering.

"The workshop is in ruins," she told Elijah.

He shook his head. "The boy took me there on our way home this evening. The structure is solid. The repairs are certainly not beyond the skills of a pair of boatbuilders."

"But the supplies, the clay and the tools and—"

He stopped her with a raised hand. "Those things would need to be addressed, but first you must decide whether or not you're agreeable to the arrangement."

Danel had stopped his work to watch her. The more she considered the idea, the more appealing it became. They may not be accepted in Zarephath, but the bulk of the pottery made in the village was sold elsewhere. In more accepting regions, like Sidon and Judah and even Egypt, being two women in partnership might work to their favor.

"We do have an extra room upstairs." A thought occurred to her, and she frowned. "But how will I feed two more? Yahweh's grain and oil are sufficient to feed us, but no more."

"Has the Lord my God not promised to supply grain and oil for you and your household?" Elijah's piercing gaze held hers. "He will not fail to provide all that you require, even if that household expands."

He spoke with such certainty that Adaliah believed him. How could she not, when every morning she dipped her hand into the grain jar and was reminded anew of his God's promise to her?

"Then let a message be sent to Kinneret," she said. "Tomorrow I will clear out an upstairs room in preparation for our guests."

It was only after Danel and Elijah were asleep on their pallets and Adaliah made her nightly journey to the well that she thought of Tanytha. What would she say when she learned that another couple was living in the house she considered hers, and the woman not only with child but working the kiln that had belonged to her abba?

Shemen's family must have packed up and left the moment they received word. Four weeks after Adaliah agreed to accept them into her home, a cart rolled through the streets of Zarephath. By the time it stopped in front of her house, it had picked up a small crowd of curious spectators.

She opened the door to find a couple waiting outside. The man looked so much like his brother, at first glance Adaliah thought it was Shemen. But this man was younger by a few years, she guessed, and leaner than the muscular boatbuilder.

"Adaliah, widow of Itthobaal?" he asked, and then continued without waiting for an answer. "I am Eban ben Nabat. My brother is Shemen."

"Of that I have no doubt." She smiled into eyes identical to her friend's, and then switched her gaze to his wife.

The young woman standing before her was several years her husband's junior, probably not more than seventeen. Adaliah's spirits sank. Surely, she hadn't had time to develop much skill as a potter if she were no older than that. Still, what had Adaliah expected? She herself had been that age when she married, and Danel born not a year later. The news that the couple was expecting their first child should have told her Shemen's sister-in-law would be young.

"This is my wife." Eban put an arm around his wife's shoulders and pulled her forward, his chest swelling with pride. "Her name is Gabrielle, but she prefers to be called Brielle."

"Welcome." Adaliah extended her hands. "I hope we shall be friends."

Brielle smiled, revealing a pair of appealing dimples. She took Adaliah's hands and squeezed them. "I am sure we will."

Adaliah glanced at the cart behind them, which was pulled by a donkey. In the cart's center stood a potter's wheel, its shape unmistakable to anyone who lived in Zarephath. Other items had been tucked in around it.

"If you'd like to bring your things inside, I'll show you where to put them."

A man standing at the animal's head dropped the lead and headed toward the back. Eban went to help him unload their belongings. Before Adaliah went inside, she scanned the faces of the onlookers. Keprea stood among them, an eager light in her eyes as she watched the men begin to untie the ropes that held the wheel in place.

Tanytha would get word of Adaliah's new houseguests before nightfall.

Adaliah rose early the next morning. Her dreams had been full of doubt, and her rest fitful. What if Elijah was wrong? What if she had to stretch her daily allotment of flour that had filled three bellies into enough to feed five? Moving as silently as she could, she crept from the bedchamber and approached her worktable. She took the grain jar from the shelf and set it on the surface. For a moment she stood staring at it.

*Please…*

The silent prayer held all her anxiety, all her doubt. And as much hope as she could muster.

She plunged her hand inside.

The jar was nearly full.

# CHAPTER NINETEEN

Adaliah picked up the ash-covered remnants of a pitcher and fitted two pieces together. "I haven't done anything with it," she told the others. "It isn't easy, coming back here."

She stood in the middle of the workshop with Shemen, Eban, Brielle, and Danel. Elijah had excused himself from the inspection, saying he wanted to spend time in prayer. Brielle had been ecstatic over the kiln, declaring it much finer than the one her cousin had inherited from their grandfather. But now, standing among the charred remains of what had once been a thriving and successful pottery business, she had fallen silent. The stench of stale smoke permeated everything and seeped into the fabric of their clothing. Above them, a small flock of gulls perched atop the soot-covered walls, watching them. The birds had moved into the deserted building and were not happy to have their home invaded.

"Of course it isn't." Brielle laid a comforting hand on Adaliah's arm. "I can't imagine."

Her voice held so much sympathy that Adaliah's eyes prickled with unshed tears. The woman misunderstood her statement, but that was to be expected. How could she know that it was not grief but guilt that nearly choked her every time her gaze fell on the place where Itthobaal had lain, trapped and demanding that she help him?

Eban pointed toward a beam that, though singed, still stretched from the top of one wall to the other. "That will need to come down. And we might stretch a tent across the opening until we can rebuild the roof."

Shemen laughed. "I don't think we need to worry about rain."

"Only bird droppings," his brother replied. He peeked through the entrance to the small storage room. "There are still a few supplies in here. I wonder if the stains are usable."

"I don't see why not." Brielle joined him and then nodded. "They're securely covered, and this wall would have protected them from the worst of the heat." She turned back to survey the rubble. "We're a long way from needing them, though. We have a lot of cleaning to do first."

Eban's expression grew stern. "You must leave the heavy lifting to us." He placed a protective arm around her shoulders. "I won't have you endangering my son."

Though she'd confided to Adaliah that her baby's arrival was still at least four months off, without her travel robe Brielle's swelling belly was obvious.

"It won't take long to clear this away." Shemen picked up a blackened chunk of wood and tossed it through the open doorway.

A female exclamation from outside answered the thud of the wood when it hit the ground. Startled, Shemen rushed to the doorway. When he turned once again to face them, he wore a guarded expression. His eyes met Adaliah's.

"Your stepdaughter is here."

Inwardly, Adaliah cringed. Truly, she had expected Tanytha to barge into the house last night and demand to know the meaning of the strangers' arrival. At least they'd been given a night's reprieve. She hurried through the doorway, hoping to spare the newcomers an unpleasant encounter.

"What is this?" Tanytha's sharp tone no doubt carried into the shop. "Who are these people?"

Adaliah had planned her response. "They're my new boarders," she answered smoothly.

"Is the Hebrew gone?"

"No." She offered no further explanation.

"Hello." Brielle appeared in the doorway and displayed her dimples by way of greeting.

After one measured look, Tanytha averted her gaze. Brielle's obvious pregnancy was no doubt painful for her to see. She kept her gaze on Adaliah. "I'm told they arrived with a potter's wheel."

Adaliah opened her mouth to answer, but Brielle was faster. "It belonged to my grandfather. Now it is mine."

Tanytha grabbed Adaliah by the arm and pulled her around to the other side of the kiln.

"What have you done?" she spat. "You haven't sold my abba's kiln, have you?"

Rubbing her arm, Adaliah shook her head. "No. As I told Resheph, the kiln is Danel's inheritance from *his* abba."

Outrage flashed onto Tanytha's face but disappeared almost as quickly, replaced by a look of utter confusion. "You told Resheph?"

"Yes, when he offered to buy the kiln I told him it was not for sale. I've said the same to everyone."

Tanytha took a backward step. "You lie. Why would Resheph want to buy a kiln?"

*She doesn't know.* Adaliah digested this information, her conversation with Resheph replaying itself in her mind. "He said he had been training with Itthobaal for a while and preferred the work of a potter to that of a dye maker. His offer was to buy the kiln and the house."

She watched a series of emotions play across the woman's features. That she was surprised, even shocked, was clear. But something else lurked in the troubled eyes fixed on Adaliah.

"Did he not tell you?" she asked.

The question seemed to jerk Tanytha out of her thoughts. "Why are these people here?" She waved a hand toward the workshop.

Not an answer, but Adaliah judged it best not to press the point. Let Tanytha question her husband if she wanted to know his plans.

Though she would prefer not to discuss their arrangement until the shop was cleaned and repaired, and she could see a sample of Brielle's work, she couldn't think of a satisfactory answer except the truth.

Bracing herself for a heated response, she said, "Brielle hopes to become a potter. She is going to help me get the business going again."

Instead of launching into another verbal attack, Tanytha flinched as if warding off a blow. Her eyes swam with unshed tears. Adaliah could have withstood a heated reply, but the sight of those tears wrenched her heart.

"I'm sorry," she said, though why she should apologize she didn't know. "I—I would have told you if—"

But Tanytha didn't wait to hear her explanation. She whirled and stumbled away, leaving Adaliah to stare after her.

The days settled into a pattern. In the mornings Adaliah rose before anyone else to stoke the cook fire and grind Yahweh's grain into flour for the day's bread. Though she couldn't explain why, she was hesitant for Brielle to discover the miracle of the grain and oil. Judging by their conversations it was clear that Shemen remained unaware of Elijah's true name, so she must assume his brother and sister-in-law were equally uninformed. The first few days Brielle stumbled down the stairs, her hair disheveled and her eyes only half awake, and scolded Adaliah for not waking her to help.

"I like grinding the grain myself," Adaliah told her. "Please don't think I'm selfish, but it gives me a pleasure I don't wish to give up."

Brielle accepted the explanation, and Adaliah relaxed, her secret—*Elijah's* secret—safe.

After the morning meal, Elijah, Eban, and Danel left for the harbor. Brielle and Adaliah spent the days cleaning out the workshop, though they left the heavy lifting for the evening, when the brothers came to help. Though Adaliah offered an unused upstairs room to Shemen, he refused.

"I'll stay in my bachelor's tent," he told her. "I like to be near my boat, just to make sure no one disturbs it in the night."

Brielle endeared herself to Adaliah with her sunny outlook on virtually everything.

"Look here," she told Adaliah one day about a week after her arrival.

Adaliah swept a pile of ash through the doorway before turning. Brielle's eyes sparkled, her hands cradling a pile of unknown objects—unknown, at least, to Adaliah.

"What are they?"

"Tools." She picked up a thin strand of metal attached to wooden handles on each end. "This is a clay cutter. And this." She held out an object that resembled a stylus. "This is a carving needle."

Though Adaliah saw nothing to justify such excitement, she couldn't help but smile.

"I found them wrapped in an oiled cloth in the storage room, along with hardwood ribs and trimming tools. They are finely crafted, the tools of a master potter. It's a wonder they weren't destroyed in the fire." Her grin deepened. "I think this is a sign of Yahweh's blessing on our business."

No one could spend more than a few minutes around Brielle without knowing she worshipped the Hebrew God. His name was on her lips a dozen times an hour. Adaliah had never met anyone who spoke of the gods with such devotion.

She hid a smile at the idea of Itthobaal's reaction if he could hear that his tools were being interpreted as a sign from a foreign God.

"I'm sure you'll make good use of them," she said.

Brielle drew in a sudden breath. Her eyes widened, and the tools dropped to the dirt at her feet, forgotten.

"Quick, Addie, feel him." She grabbed Adaliah's hands and placed them on her round belly.

Startled as much by the nickname as by Brielle's actions, Adaliah almost drew back. But then she felt the movements of the babe. Memories rushed back to her, of her awe and delight when she felt Danel quicken in her womb.

She laughed. "This one is going to be a lively child for sure, boy or girl."

"Oh, he's a boy," Brielle said with certainty. "Eban and I have both prayed for a boy, and I know Yahweh hears our prayers."

Adaliah kept her doubts to herself. Instead, she picked up the forgotten tools and handed them back.

"What did you call me?" she asked.

"Oh!" Two spots of color surfaced on the smooth cheeks. "It's a habit of my family to shorten people's names. I didn't mean to be disrespectful."

"No, I..." Adaliah fell silent. A memory from long ago surged forward, more an impression of a kind smile and warm arms and a soft voice crooning in her ear. "My wet nurse called me Addie. I'd forgotten."

"You had a wet nurse?" Brielle asked. "Were you rich?"

An acerbic laugh blasted from Adaliah's lips. "Hardly. My mother—" She swallowed a surge of guilt. "My mother died in childbirth."

The color in Brielle's face drained, and Adaliah realized what she'd said. She pulled Brielle into her arms. "Don't be afraid. That won't happen to you."

A sound from behind broke into the moment. Releasing Brielle, she turned to find Badahur standing in the doorway. His gaze circled the room and then rested for a moment on Brielle.

"I didn't believe it." He looked at Adaliah. "I heard you had started a boardinghouse for displaced Hebrews, but I thought they were joking. And you've hired a woman to run your shop?"

Scorn dripped from his tone, which rendered Brielle uncharacteristically silent.

An icy finger of fear traced its way up Adaliah's spine. If word had spread through Zarephath that she was housing Hebrews, how long would it be before someone wondered if one of them might be the prophet of the drought?

She suppressed a chill and lifted her chin. "Not hired. We're going into business together as partners."

He stared at her for another moment, and his gaze dropped to take in Brielle's belly. His lips twisted into a sneer, and then he started to laugh. The mocking guffaws resounded off the walls, filling the confines of the workshop and sending fire into Adaliah's face. She stiffened her spine, casting about for a comment that would silence the insulting laughter. Before she could settle on an appropriate barb, he turned and left, still laughing.

When the offensive sound had faded into the distance, Brielle whispered, "Who was that?"

Several moments passed before Adaliah conquered the panic that threatened to rob her of breath. She drew air deeply into her lungs and blew it out before answering.

"A rival." She put on a confident smile that she did not feel. "No one who matters."

# CHAPTER TWENTY

Elijah halted at the doorway of the house where Yahweh had hidden him away. He rested a hand on the doorpost and closed his eyes. Though the Lord was ever with him—a presence he perceived more than felt in his spirit—sometimes he felt compelled to seek solitude so he could enjoy a deeper communion without the distraction of others.

"Is something wrong?"

Danel's question pierced through his thoughts, which brought the need for a few hours' seclusion more clearly into focus. Shemen and Eban had gone directly to the pottery workshop after their day's work on the boat was finished, and he had accompanied the boy home.

He smiled at the child. "Nothing is wrong. You go on inside and tell your imma I will be home late. Ask her to save a bite to eat from the evening meal."

"Where are you going?" The boy's eyes lit. "Can I come with you?"

"Not this time." He watched disappointment douse the child's enthusiasm. Removing his hand from the doorframe, he then rested it on Danel's head. "Sometimes a man must be alone with the Lord."

After a moment's careful consideration, Danel nodded and disappeared inside the house.

Elijah wandered through the streets, following an inner nudge that he had long ago learned to recognize. The day was drawing to an end, and he saw more than one shop owner pull his shutters closed. He nodded a greeting to those who met his eye, but they were few.

"This is not a friendly village You have sent me to," he whispered.

The answer was a feeling, a wash of divine sorrow that flooded his heart. Yahweh loved all people, and their wayward lives saddened Him. If only they could feel what He allowed Elijah to feel, the longing with which their Creator wished to gather them to Him as a mother gathers her children. Once Elijah had believed that Yahweh's heart beat only for His chosen people, but now he knew better. The children of Israel were set apart to be an example to the nations of His love and care, a love that He longed to extend to any who sought Him.

A bitter memory arose. When the Lord sent Elijah to confront the king of the northern kingdom, Ahab had laughed with scorn at the judgment of God. A poorer example of God's chosen had never lived.

Elijah turned a corner and stopped. Before him lay the pagan temple. In the center of the courtyard rose an Asherah pole, a grotesque depiction of a faceless woman in a seductive pose. The sight turned his stomach, and the smoke rising from an altar somewhere inside the elaborate building nauseated him. The shrieks of the priests and those they led in worship so disgusted him that he clapped his hands over his ears and turned away.

Again, a nearly overwhelming sense of sorrow washed over him as he hurried away from the vile place. What would become of those who were taken in by the evil that Jezebel had spread throughout the land?

He plunged through the village gates, guided by an inner urge to put the place as far behind him as he could. Though the plain beckoned him with its wide-open spaces that bore no stain of any man, his feet took him through one olive grove after another. Finally, when the buildings of Zarephath had long since disappeared behind him, he stopped. He had arrived, whatever that meant. Selecting a sturdy tree, he dropped to the ground beneath its branches and sat with his legs folded and his arms resting on his knees. No wind stirred the branches above him, and the only sounds were the chirps of insects. He closed his eyes and waited. The sun disappeared, and the air around him grew chilly.

The Presence swelled within him.

*Elijah.*

"I am here, my Lord," he whispered the answer.

*You will celebrate Passover with the household of the widow to whom I have sent you.*

The words surprised him. Of course he had known Passover was a few days away, but in this heathen city he had resigned himself to observing the sacred day alone, without the accompanying traditions. The Lord knew his heart and knew he would keep Passover there.

He opened his mouth, thoughts vying with each other to be spoken first. But the certainty of the Lord's command left no room for dispute. The logistics of the sacred holiday were far beyond his ability to arrange. But he knew by now that Yahweh could arrange anything He chose.

"Yes, my Lord," he replied. Then added a question. "How?"

A sound pulled his attention from the Divine to his surroundings. He opened his eyes to scan the area around him. The sound continued, like the mewling cries of an infant, only not quite. He caught sight of the source, and a joyful laugh bubbled up from the depths of his soul.

A lamb stood not more than a cubit away, its snowy white wool shining in a ray of moonlight that filtered through the branches above. Elijah got to his feet and approached the creature with an outstretched hand, still chuckling. The lamb stood still, even when he stroked its soft wool, which had grown long enough to lose some of its curl. The length and texture confirmed the lamb's age—one year. Of course it would be one year. Jehovah Jireh, the Divine Provider, knew the required age better than any one, since He had specified it Himself.

Elijah gathered the animal into his arms and headed back to Zarephath.

# CHAPTER TWENTY-ONE

Adaliah traced a letter in their makeshift tablet. "That is *daleth*." She handed the stick to Danel. "Can you make that one?"

From her mat in the corner of the courtyard Brielle looked up from her sewing and smiled at Danel. Eban had retired shortly after their evening meal, tired from a long day of work. If they listened closely, they could hear the sounds of his soft snore coming from the window of the upstairs room that had become their bedchamber.

The door leading into the house opened, and they all looked up. When Elijah stepped into the courtyard carrying a lamb, Danel dropped the stick and leaped to his feet.

"What is this?" He rushed forward and ran his fingers across the lamb's wool.

"I assume you recognize a young sheep when you see one." Elijah's lips twisted with humor. "Therefore, the real question becomes *why are you bringing a lamb into the house?*"

Adaliah picked up the abandoned tray and set it to one side, her thoughts troubled. Where had Elijah gotten a lamb? That it was meant to be an addition to their meal tray was clear, for the animal was too young to give milk and too small to provide enough wool to be useful. She glanced at the place where she had buried Boz. Her only experience at slaughtering an animal for its meat left her with no desire to do it again.

Danel rubbed one short ear. "He won't stay in the house, will he?" He gave her a questioning glance over one shoulder.

She opened her mouth to answer, "Certainly not," but Elijah spoke first.

"Oh yes. For four days he will stay with us."

"A Pesach lamb." Brielle put aside her sewing and got to her feet. She caressed the lamb's neck. "My father always takes me with him to go through the shepherd's flock and find a perfect one."

"This one was selected by Yahweh Himself."

Elijah set the creature on the ground. Danel dropped to his knees before the animal, and it bleated softly.

Delight broke out on the child's face. "What shall we name him? And can he sleep with me?"

Adaliah found her voice. "Animals do not live in houses," she told them all in a voice that left no room for argument. "Not even for a short time."

Danel's features fell, and Brielle shot a quick glance in her direction. A look passed between Brielle and Elijah before she excused herself and disappeared into the house.

Elijah came to sit beside Adaliah. "Did your grandmother never speak to you of Passover?"

She was spared answering when Danel asked, "What is Passover?"

"It is a sacred holiday celebrated by every Hebrew in the month of Nissan. We commemorate the deliverance of our people from persecution and slavery in the land of Egypt."

The lamb wandered across the courtyard, investigating its new surroundings. Entranced, Danel followed behind it.

Adaliah did remember her grandmother talking of that particular celebration, and once had even roasted a lamb in the family's oven, though she spoke to no one of the significance of the day except Adaliah.

"Danel." Her voice cut across the courtyard, sharper than she intended. He turned with a question on his face. "That animal is not a pet. It is livestock, just as Boz was. Do you understand?"

Realization flashed onto his face, and he turned a troubled expression to Elijah. "Are you going to eat him?"

The prophet answered with a dip of his forehead. "Passover is five days from now, and yes, the special meal includes a spotless lamb."

Tears filled the child's eyes, and he drew a shuddering breath before turning his back. The lamb, oblivious to its fate, frolicked across the open area to sniff at the trunk of the olive tree.

She rounded on Elijah, angry on behalf of her son. "Where did you get it? And why could you not leave it there until the time came to have it slaughtered?"

If she thought her words would rouse the prophet, she was wrong. He answered in a tender voice.

"The Lord my God instructed His children to select a lamb without blemish, and to take it into their homes for four days before Passover. That is so we have ample time to think of the meaning of the sacrifice we are about to make."

"Then your God is cruel," she snapped.

His voice became even softer. "No. He is full of compassion. He knows our sorrows and suffers with us, just as you feel your own child's heartache."

Danel's back was still turned toward them, but his shoulders heaved with a suppressed sob. Adaliah leaped up from her cushion and gathered him close. She pulled him gently toward the house.

"We've had enough sacrifice in this family," she told Elijah without turning. "I will not bring that animal into my house. You're welcome to sleep out here, in the courtyard, and think about the meaning of *your* sacrifice."

His voice stopped her just before she crossed the threshold.

"If that is your wish," he said in a mild tone. "But may we at least remove that offensive idol from the presence of the lamb?"

Anger burned like a flame in her blood. Was the prophet of the drought bent on turning her house into a Hebrew refuge? Did he have no fear that someone would report him, and that Jezebel's troops would show up at her door and kill them all? She turned her head to look at the ugly image of Baal. While she had no love for the god, its presence proved that she was no Hebrew.

"The statue stays," she said without turning, and then left Elijah with his lamb.

For the next four days Adaliah avoided the courtyard. She left the care of Elijah's lamb to Brielle, who remained silent on the matter. When the young woman offered to prepare the special Passover meal, Adaliah conceded with a nod. She'd half expected to find the grain jar empty the morning after her outburst and felt a twinge of remorse when Yahweh proved faithful once again.

The day of the holiday arrived. Adaliah rose early, as was her custom, but found Brielle already awake and standing before her worktable.

"Good morning," she said in a singsong voice when Adaliah emerged from her bedchamber. "I left the grinding for you since I know you enjoy it."

It was impossible to remain sour in the face of Brielle's eternal cheerfulness. Adaliah drew near to take down the jar of grain and looked in her bowl. Brielle worked with a knife, chopping nuts.

"What is that?" Adaliah asked.

"It's a dish my mother always makes on Passover. Hers has nuts, apples, pears, and a little wine. But we have no pears and no wine." She shrugged. "I've made do with water."

When they arrived, the couple had unloaded several bundles of foodstuffs. Adaliah nearly wept when they offered them freely for the household meals. Conscious of the increasing drought, Adaliah rationed the supplies with rigid control. Judging by the ingredients laid out before Brielle now, she guessed that rationing was to be thrown to the wind today. The celebration would include an extravagant meal.

"Danel will love it," she said.

"I hope so." Brielle giggled. "I can't wait to see his face when he eats the herbs. Oh Addie, they're the most bitter things you've ever put in your mouth."

She pulled a face that made Adaliah laugh.

"Why would you eat them, then?"

Brielle shrugged. "It's a tradition commanded by the Lord."

"What a strange custom." Adaliah took the grain jar to her quern.

"It's supposed to remind us of the bitterness of the slavery our ancestors suffered." Brielle continued her chopping as she spoke. "And we dip vegetables in saltwater to recall their tears. And there's the lamb, of course."

She fell silent at the mention of the source of conflict in the household.

Adaliah spread grain on the quern and picked up her grinding stone. "I don't understand the purpose of the lamb," she confessed.

Brielle continued chopping for a moment. Then she put the knife down and turned to lean her back against the worktable.

"Lambs were sacred to the Egyptians. Yahweh knew that having the Hebrew people, whom they thought of as slaves, sacrifice a lamb would be offensive. Our tradition calls the sacrifice an abomination in the eyes of Egypt."

Adaliah chose her next words with care so as not to offend the young woman who had become her friend. "Why did Yahweh purposefully provoke them?"

"Because Moses had asked Pharaoh over and over to set the Hebrews free. The Egyptians were afflicted with boils and locusts and other plagues, but Pharaoh still refused." She shook her head, her face a mask of sorrow. "If only the insult of taking their sacred animal into their homes for days with the intent of slaughtering it had convinced Pharaoh, many Egyptian lives would have been saved."

That story, at least, Adaliah remembered in detail. The firstborn of every Egyptian family died. She shuddered. Her firstborn was Danel.

A bleating cry out in the courtyard drew her attention. She paused in her work to look in that direction. Today might be a holiday for some, but for the animal it was a day of death. Her stomach turned at the thought that her courtyard would once again see the grizzly sight of an animal's slaughter.

She looked at Brielle. "Who will…prepare the meat?"

"Elijah. At twilight." An understanding smile flashed onto her face. "I think Danel should stay inside and help us with the rest of the meal at that time."

Adaliah nodded. An excellent idea.

The time for the Passover feast drew near. Adaliah kept Danel close to her side at twilight, when Elijah, Shemen, and Eban filed out into the courtyard. He sat on his cushion in a circle of lamplight tracing letters in the sand.

"Don't be sad, Imma," he had told her that afternoon when the men returned home from the shore. "Johanan told me why the lamb must be killed."

Her jaw tightened, but she filtered the tension out of her voice. "Did he? What did he say?"

"The lamb proves to Yahweh that we love Him better than anything. And the lamb has to be perfect, because Yahweh's love for us is perfect."

Adaliah recalled his words as she watched her son bend over the sand. The child's unquestioning acceptance of Elijah's explanation both calmed and disturbed her. He had grown increasingly fond of the prophet. What would happen when Elijah left? Or if the worst happened, if he was discovered and killed by Jezebel's soldiers? If she could only spare Danel the heartache of another loss.

Brielle bustled into the house from the courtyard. "The meal is nearly ready. Danel, will you call the others?"

Nodding, he put the tray to one side and headed for the stairway. Elijah had retired to his room to pray, while Shemen and Eban sat on the roof discussing their plans for the boats they would build together.

"I couldn't find the right herbs," Brielle told Adaliah when the boy had gone upstairs. "I know I brought some from home, but I must have tucked them away somewhere. But I have the perfect substitute." She grinned. "Green olives."

Adaliah made a face. "If bitter is what you want, that will certainly work."

They were interrupted by a rap on the outside door. The sound set Adaliah's pulse racing. But surely soldiers would not knock politely. Drying her damp palms on her tunic, she calmed herself before opening the door.

Outside she found Tanytha and Resheph standing in the darkened street. Tanytha wore her usual pinched expression, and even Resheph looked stern.

"We've come to talk with you about the kiln," he said in a flat voice.

Adaliah bit back a sigh. She should have foreseen this visit.

Shooting a glance over her shoulder where her Hebrew houseguests were ready to begin their holy celebration, she told them, "Now is not a good time."

Elijah approached to stand beside her. "Greetings." He nodded at Tanytha and then smiled at Resheph. "I am called Johanan."

Watching Elijah through narrowed eyes, Resheph mumbled his name.

Adaliah turned a forced smile on the prophet. "They want to discuss my plans for the workshop and kiln. I was just telling them that conversation would have to wait for another time."

"We are about to have a celebration, you see," Elijah told them.

Resheph looked even more suspicious. "What sort of celebration?"

"Today is a sacred Hebrew holiday called Passover." His expression brightened. "Perhaps you'd like to join us."

Adaliah's jaw went slack. Had the prophet lost his mind?

Tanytha placed a hand on her husband's arm and shook her head. Good. At least someone had sense.

"We have plenty," Elijah said, adding in a tempting tone, "and the women have been cooking all day."

Adaliah would have voiced a protest, but just then her mouth was drier than a desert.

Resheph held the prophet's eye for a long moment before nodding. "Thank you for the gracious invitation. We accept."

Then it was Tanytha's turn to stare slack-jawed, at Resheph. "We do?"

"Why not? Besides"—he inhaled a deep breath—"something smells good."

Adaliah noticed afresh the aroma of roasting meat wafting from the direction of the courtyard.

"Excellent." Elijah beamed and stepped back, gesturing them into the house as if he were its master. He announced to those inside, "We have guests to help us celebrate the Passover."

When the couple entered, Adaliah glared at the prophet over their heads. In response, he gave her an angelic smile and followed them.

Though Adaliah would have liked to fume throughout the formal recitation before the meal, she found herself strangely intrigued as Elijah recounted the story of Joseph, who emerged from a prison cell to become a mighty man in Egypt. Perhaps no one but she knew the reason for the emotion in the prophet's voice when he described the drought that gripped Egypt at that time and spurred Joseph's rise to power. She listened, enthralled, as he spoke of the conditions under which the

Hebrews struggled generations afterward, and how Yahweh chose Moses to lead them to freedom.

They ate in the courtyard, seated in a circle. She noted that the statue of Baal had been moved, tucked into a corner where it lay shrouded in shadows. Had Tanytha not been present Adaliah might have mentioned the fact that she had not been consulted, but she didn't want to draw the woman's attention to it.

The meal mat between them held a true feast, one that made Tanytha's eyes bulge when she sat on the cushion Brielle set down for her. Resheph, normally talkative, sat beside her and watched the proceedings in silence. Their only light was from candles on the mat and from the moon and stars above them.

When they were all seated, Danel eyed the abundance of food arrayed before him. "Why is this meal different than other meals?"

Elijah answered with an indulgent smile. "Because we were slaves to Pharaoh in Egypt, and the Lord our God took us out from there with a strong hand and an outstretched arm. This night we remember that deliverance."

He explained the symbolism of the saltwater into which he dipped a potato slice and encouraged them to do the same. When the tang of salt hit Adaliah's tongue, she shut her eyes. She had certainly tasted enough tears in her lifetime to make the parallel real to her.

"We also eat bitter herbs in remembrance of the bitterness of slavery." Elijah picked up a dish of uncured olives, took one, and then passed the bowl to Shemen. "The herbs are missing from tonight's meal, but the Lord our God understands our circumstances."

When everyone had taken an olive, Elijah bit into his and immediately tears filled his eyes. Danel held his in his hand and stared at it, his reluctance plain.

Beside him, Shemen sank his teeth into the olive and his features puckered. "*Eewwweee!* I never thought I'd wish for some of those herbs, but they'd taste like honey compared to this."

His exclamation, and Danel's answering giggle, broke the solemn mood. Adaliah chuckled along with everyone, and nibbled a bit of the sour fruit. Resheph, she noticed, did not, but to her surprise Tanytha partook.

When everyone had gulped water to clear their mouths and Brielle had refilled their cups, Elijah picked up a large wafer of bread. Brielle had insisted on cooking the dough until it was dry and crisp, explaining only that it was their tradition.

Elijah lifted the wafer toward the sky. "Blessed be You, Lord our God, King of the world, who brings bread out of the earth."

*Or out of an earthen jar.* Adaliah's lips twitched with a suppressed giggle at the thought.

He snapped the wafer into two and then turned a wide grin on Danel. "Now we may eat our fill."

The feast began. The courtyard rang with happy chatter and laughter as they ate, the mood one of real celebration. Brielle's contagious giggle flowed freely, and Eban proved himself as adept at storytelling as his brother.

Though Resheph and Tanytha ate as much as anyone, Adaliah noted that they did not join in the festive chatter.

# CHAPTER TWENTY-TWO

The days following the Passover feast passed without incident, though Adaliah could not escape a sense of looming
trouble. She kept her worries to herself but not, apparently, as
tightly guarded as she thought. One morning as they were
clearing the remains of their meal after the men had gone to
the shore, Brielle confronted her.

"Addie, what's wrong?" The young woman stood with her
hands cradling her belly.

"What could be wrong?" Adaliah averted her gaze, intent
on straightening the bowls on the shelf beneath her worktable.

"You've been too quiet, and you jump at the slightest noise.
I know you're worried about something."

At times Adaliah got lost in Brielle's lighthearted manner and forgot that she could be unusually astute. She turned
her back under the guise of shaking the crumbs off the meal
mat.

"Are you having second thoughts about our pottery business?" Brielle asked.

"No." Adaliah dropped the mat back into place. "I wish we
could get started sooner. I'm impatient."

"I'm glad you haven't changed your mind." Brielle settled
herself on Danel's stool and leaned back against the wall. "But

it does seem like there's something else bothering you. I wish you'd confide in me."

Her tone held a plaintive request, but Adaliah was rescued from answering by someone pounding on the door. The sound rang in the enclosed room. An answering thud began in her chest. With a quick glance at Brielle, she hurried to open the door. When she recognized the man outside, her heart stuttered.

"Fayez," she managed to croak through a dry throat.

The chief priest wore his official robes, intricate designs in gold thread etched down the front of the crimson cloth. From his neck hung a heavy chain with a pendent shaped in the hideous likeness of Baal. Her gaze flickered to his hands, which were thankfully clean.

"I've had disturbing reports and wish to speak with you about them." He speared her with a cold gaze. "May I come in?"

This was it, the trouble she'd anticipated. Resheph and Tanytha had no doubt gone straight from the Passover meal to the temple.

In answer she dipped her head and stood aside so he could enter. When he swept past, his billowing robes released the scent of the incense used in the ceremonies he conducted. Inside, he caught sight of Brielle and stopped short. The young woman's eyes widened as she took in his elaborate costume and for once seemed too overwhelmed to speak.

"This is Fayez, who serves as chief priest in Zarephath's temple." Adaliah passed the priest to stand beside her friend.

"And this is Brielle, wife of Eban ben Nebat, recently from Kenneret." She paused. "She is my houseguest."

"A *Hebrew*." Fayez spat the word as though it were offensive.

Because Adaliah's arm was touching Brielle's she felt her shrink. A protective instinct stirred to life in Adaliah. How often had she been the target of scornful gazes, such as the priest fixed on Brielle now?

"Yes, she is Hebrew." She gave a slight shrug, as if to say *What does it matter?*

"And where are the others?" He glanced around the room as if expecting to find them hiding in the corners.

"They're working."

"Building a boat, I hear." His lips curved into a brittle smile. "Or are they working in your husband's shop today?"

Adaliah stiffened and held his eye. "They work in *my* shop in the evenings, after their daily work is finished."

He acknowledged the correction with the slightest dip of his forehead. "I'm told that you conducted a Hebrew ritual here some nights past."

Inside she quaked, but she answered evenly. "It seems you've been told a lot. But you are mistaken. I conducted nothing."

"Ah, yes." He nodded. "The ceremony was led by one of your…guests. I've forgotten his name."

Though she knew he had forgotten nothing, she supplied the name. "His name is Johanan."

"Might we speak privately?"

His gaze slid to Brielle, who slid off the stool and escaped up the stairs in a hurry, as if she'd been released from debtor's prison.

"Let's go out to the courtyard, where it's cooler," Adaliah said.

She picked up her water jug and two cups on the way. Offering hospitality would give her something to focus on. She hesitated over the covered pile of cakes she'd made this morning but decided against offering one of those. To give Yahweh's bread to a priest of Baal might offend the Hebrew God, and that was a risk she was not prepared to take.

When he was seated, Fayez studied his surroundings while Adaliah filled his cup. His gaze rested for a moment on the statue of Baal, and he gave a slight nod.

"I see you haven't completely given up our practices."

She almost replied that she had given up those practices when he refused to help her, but instead busied herself with pouring her own water and settling on her cushion.

But he wasn't prepared to let the matter pass. "I feared I might find your house as full of Hebrew relics as it is full of Hebrews."

"If you are asking if I've begun worshipping the Hebrew God, the answer is no," she replied calmly.

"That is welcome news." A chilly half smile appeared on his lips. "I shudder to imagine how the people of Zarephath would react if that were true."

"The reactions of the people of Zarephath do not concern me in the slightest." Though not completely true, she made the statement in a light tone. "If their treatment of me since the death of my husband is any indication, they will ignore me no matter what I do."

His eyes narrowed. "May I remind you that your position in this village is precarious? Many still question the cause behind Itthobaal's death."

With an effort, she stilled a violent tremble that threatened to slosh water from her cup. "His death was a tragic accident, as you yourself told me." She tightened her lips. "Though you refused to speak to anyone else on my behalf."

For a long moment he didn't reply. When he did, his voice was lighter.

"Tell me about your houseguests. Where are they from?"

The abrupt change of subject disarmed Adaliah, and she didn't answer for the span of a few breaths. Was this the real reason for the priest's visit, to question her about Elijah?

She matched his conversational tone. "Brielle, whom you've just met, and her husband are from Kinneret. Eban and his brother are both boatbuilders."

"Yes, yes, I've heard of them." He dismissed them with a flick of his fingers in the air. "What of the other one, the man who came first? I've forgotten his name again."

"Johanan." She sipped from her cup, her thoughts racing. What had she told Tanytha about Elijah's origins? She dared not contradict herself. "He is Hebrew, as you know." She gave a falsely apologetic laugh. "And no fan of our Princess Jezebel, I fear."

"Who is no longer our princess, but his queen if he comes from Israel."

"Just so," she agreed. "I've learned a lot about Hebrew beliefs in recent weeks. They hold that their God is the only True God, and all others are false. They insist that their people worship only their God and no others."

"That is absurd." The priest leaped to his feet and began to pace. "Who are Hebrews to dictate which deities we can worship? People are free to honor whichever gods they choose. Their Hebrew God, yes if they want, but to deny even the existence of Baal, Astarte, and Melqart is laughable."

Apparently Adaliah had touched upon a nerve. She'd never seen Fayez so agitated.

He stomped across the courtyard and stood before the statue of Baal. "At least you have not conformed to that intolerant attitude."

She spared a grateful thought that she had insisted on keeping the statue. Its presence in her courtyard might prove to be the factor that would enlist Zarephath's chief priest to her cause if disaster struck, and Elijah's identify were discovered. She could claim complete ignorance of the prophet's true name and nature.

Guilt stabbed like a knife to her chest, so strong it nearly robbed her of breath. Elijah and his Lord had rescued her from certain death. What did it say of her that she was ready to deny him to save herself?

*And to save Danel. My son has no one but me. I must never forget that.*

Fayez returned to her, though he did not sit. Instead, he towered over her, forcing her to crane her neck to look up at him.

"Do you know nothing else about this man, this Johanan?" A dangerous glint appeared in his eyes. "I find it odd that a Hebrew who claims to want to escape from the spread of Baal's temples in his own land would come here, to Zarephath. Are we not known for our dedication in serving that god and the others?"

Adaliah could think of no safe response. To cover her silence, she picked up his discarded cup and then got to her feet. Once she was closer to the same level as him, she looked him in the eye.

"I think you should ask Johanan himself. Most days you'll find him on the shore not far from the north harbor, helping his friends build their boat."

She signaled the end to their conversation by leaving the courtyard, hoping that he would follow.

In the following days Adaliah congratulated herself on her success in putting a stop to the chief priest's suspicions. They heard nothing further from the temple and returned to the enjoyable routine established before Passover.

Brielle insisted on sharing the household duties equally. The young woman listened quietly to Adaliah's halting explanation of the reason she visited the well late at night, her expression growing harder as the account continued. When Adaliah finished, Brielle jutted her chin out, looking so much like Danel at his most stubborn that Adaliah almost laughed.

"That must stop," she announced. "I will fetch our water from now on. And I will do it in the mornings."

Adaliah sensed that to protest would be useless. Let the young woman learn for herself how malicious the women of Zarephath could be.

At first Brielle remained silent upon returning from the daily chore, but within a few days she began to bring home snatches of village news.

"Do you know a potter named Hanibal? His wife just gave birth to their fourth son."

"How exciting for them," Adaliah replied.

Brielle nodded. "And Keprea's daughter is about to be betrothed to a cousin from Sidon. Oh, and there are no more figs to be found anywhere in the market because of the drought. Mariet says someone whose name I can't remember has ordered some from Judah, but when they arrive they'll be so expensive no one will be able to afford them."

Adaliah enjoyed listening to the young woman's chatter each day. She should have known that Brielle's cheerful nature would wear down the disagreeable women. She battled a touch of envy that Brielle so easily gained ground that was firmly denied her.

Until the morning the young woman brought home news that sent a chill through her blood.

"They say soldiers from Israel will arrive soon."

They sat in the courtyard, Adaliah mending a tear in Danel's tunic while Brielle stitched a tiny garment for her baby. In place of her customary smile, she wore a solemn frown.

Adaliah's fingers trembled so violently she dropped her needle. "Why are they coming to Zarephath?"

"They're looking for the prophet of the drought."

With an effort, Adaliah stilled her shaking hands and retrieved her needle. "I can't imagine why they think they will find him in Zarephath. There aren't many Hebrews living here."

"I know. They're going everywhere, scouring the land at King Ahab's command." She looked up from her work. "Addie, Mariet says they will visit every house where a Hebrew lives, so we should be prepared for them to come here. But I told her we have nothing to hide. There are only three of us here, four if you count Shemen. And none of us are prophets."

Adaliah didn't trust her voice, so she limited her response to a nod.

The anticipated visit came that very night.

Everyone except Elijah was seated around the courtyard, having just finished their evening meal. Shemen, who now stayed at the house more often than not, had taken possession of Danel's writing tray and was drawing a sketch of the rudder he hoped to build for their next project while Eban and Danel looked on with interest. They showed no sign of stopping soon, so Adaliah stoked the fire that provided their only light. She stole glances at her son, torn between delight that he had become so interested in boats, and concern that he was growing too fond of the Hebrew men she had introduced into their lives. Perhaps she should keep him home during the days instead of letting him join the other men on the shore.

A hammering on the door startled them all. Brielle's gaze flew to Adaliah's, her eyes round.

Taking a breath in an attempt to still her pulse, Adaliah went to the door, dusting ashes from her hands. Though she was not surprised to find three soldiers outside, the sight of their leather uniforms and the swords at their sides rendered her speechless for a moment.

The man in the center peered at her down the length of a hooked nose. "Is this the house of Adaliah, widow of Itthobaal?"

"It is." At least they had been given her name as the owner of the house. She bit back a nervous laugh. "I am Adaliah."

"I am Jaron ben Ephai." He dipped his head without taking his gaze from hers. "I am here on behalf of Ahab, King of Israel, who has tasked me with finding a prophet named Elijah."

"There is no one here called by that name." She used Elijah's careful phrasing.

The soldier's expression did not relax. "But there are Hebrews living in this house?"

"Yes, there are." Shemen came up to stand beside her. "I am Hebrew."

She nearly sank against him in relief.

The man's gaze flickered from Adaliah to Shemen and back again. "May we come in?"

A politely phrased request, though voiced in a tone as cold as the metal of which his sword was made. She stepped back and allowed the three to enter. Inside, they marched to the center of the courtyard, where Eban stood with a protective arm around his wife.

Shemen took control, for which she was grateful.

"Danel," he said to the boy, "would you please fetch Johanan from his room? I'm sure these men would like to speak with him as well as us."

While he scampered up the stairs, Jaron faced Shemen while the two soldiers with him stood a step behind him, their postures stiff. "Your name?"

"Shemen ben Nebat." He gestured toward the others. "This is my brother Eban and his wife, Brielle."

"Where is your home?" Jaron asked.

"Zarephath, for now." Shemen smiled. "But our family's home is Kinneret, in Israel."

"And what is your business here?"

Shemen launched into a lengthy description of their boat-building venture and detailed a list of reasons those boats must be built on the shores of the Great Sea instead of the Lake of Galilee. Adaliah stopped listening when Elijah appeared at the top of the stairs, Danel at his side. The flames from their fire cast them in a flickering orange light. The prophet scanned the scene below, and then his gaze rested on Adaliah. Though the distance and the dim lighting hid his expression from her, he gave her a calm nod before descending.

From where she stood, she could clearly see Jaron's face. Had she not been watching, and had he not been standing close to the fire, she would have missed the widening of his eyes when he caught sight of Elijah.

*He knows.*

Her head felt light, and she wavered on her feet. They were about to die. Every instinct told her to snatch Danel and run, but fear had turned her legs to stone.

"You are the one they call Johanan?" Jaron asked.

"I am."

"And what is your business in Zarephath?"

"At present I am helping my friends build a boat."

How could he smile so broadly and speak so easily? Adaliah could not have uttered a squeak.

The soldier studied Elijah for a long moment. Then he turned to the others and barked in an official tone, "Report back to the temple and get the location of the other Hebrews. I will follow shortly."

The two acknowledged the command and, turning on their heels, left the house.

The moment the door closed behind them, Jaron dropped to his knees before the prophet, his head bowed. "My lord Elijah."

Adaliah's jaw went slack. A quick glance showed her that Shemen, Eban, and Brielle were even more astonished than she. Only Danel and Elijah himself seemed unfazed.

Danel approached the soldier and peered down at him where he knelt. "We're to call him Johanan," he said, his tone faintly scolding.

Jaron smiled at the child. "And you must continue to do so."

He rose, and Elijah embraced him. "How are you, my friend? And what news of Obadiah?"

"Wait." Shemen approached the pair. "Do you mean you are the prophet? The one all of Israel has been looking for?"

Elijah spread his hands. "The same."

Jaron rounded on Shemen. "You must never mention that again." He glared in turn at Eban, Brielle, and finally Adaliah. "To do so will bring about not only his death, but yours as well."

Brielle's hands flew to her belly, and Eban's arm tightened around her shoulders.

"The Lord my God will guard our lives." Elijah's voice held not a hint of doubt, but then his shoulders drooped. "My friend, is it true that I am the last of Yahweh's prophets left alive?"

"The king and queen believe so." A smile curved Jaron's lips. "But Obadiah has secreted one hundred of the faithful away. They are safe."

Elijah embraced the soldier again, this time thumping his leather-covered back.

"Who is Obadiah?" Danel asked.

"He is a trusted official in Ahab's palace," Jaron said.

Elijah nodded. "And he is a devout believer in Yahweh."

Adaliah's head swam to comprehend all the surprises this conversation had revealed. One thing was certain. Jaron might be Ahab's soldier, but he was no threat to Elijah or to the rest of her household.

"Sir," she said, "would you sit and talk with us? Let me give you something to eat and drink."

But Jaron shook his head. "I must get on with my search before my soldiers become suspicious of my time spent here."

He faced Elijah again. "I vow before the Lord our God that word of your location will not pass my lips. I will take your secret to my grave."

Elijah grasped the man's shoulders. "May that be a very long time coming, my friend."

When Jaron had left, Shemen folded his arms across his chest and leveled a stern stare on the prophet. "Would you like to explain?"

The prophet smiled. "What I would *like* is to return to my prayers. Our hostess can answer your questions."

With a wink at Adaliah, he ascended the stairs and disappeared into his room.

# CHAPTER TWENTY-THREE

Adaliah lifted her gaze from the mat she was weaving for their workshop when Brielle returned from the well, the jug balanced on her shoulder. The babe had grown large in recent weeks, and the young woman's belly had begun to resemble a large melon. Water sloshed over the jar's narrow lip when she set it on the worktable. In place of her habitual smile, this morning Brielle wore a scowl.

Not long ago any break from the routine would have sent Adaliah's pulse racing, but since the soldiers' visit, she'd learned to trust, if not in Elijah's God, at least in Elijah's confidence.

"Guess who I met today," Brielle said.

"Someone disagreeable, judging by your frown."

"I would sooner describe her as rude and annoying." She filled a cup with water and drank deeply before continuing. "Her name is Farah."

The name perfectly explained the reason for the scowl. "Her husband is Uday, the brother of Resheph."

"That's the one." Brielle drained her cup. "She offended Mariet with an insult about the flavor of her husband's oil, and when Keprea spoke up in her defense, Farah told her the fault might lie instead in the container in which the oil was stored, which was made by Keprea's husband. And you should have seen her expression when someone told her I was to be Zarephath's newest potter." She rolled her eyes toward the sky. "How I wish the men would finish our shop so we can show everyone what we can do."

Adaliah wished the same. Most of the rubble had been cleared from the shop, but work on the roof had not yet commenced. Shemen's boat was nearly finished, and the men focused their efforts on that, even bringing lamps to the shore to work after sunset most nights.

"Was Tanytha with her?" Adaliah asked.

She had not seen her stepdaughter in weeks, not since the Passover feast. Though her absence provided a welcome reprieve from snide comments about the ownership of the house, Adaliah couldn't help but wonder at the reason. Was she disappointed that the visit from King Ahab's soldiers didn't result in Adaliah losing her houseguests and a resulting return to her poverty-stricken state?

Brielle shook her head. "No, but Keprea did ask after her. It seems Resheph has gone on a lengthy sea voyage at his father's request. He's learning where to find the mollusks they use to make their purple dye, so he can take over that part of their business. Since he left, Farah said Tanytha mopes about the house and rarely leaves their bedchamber." She wrinkled her nose. "I don't think she likes Tanytha much. Or anyone else, it seems."

Adaliah digested the news. Tanytha was no doubt miserable living with Resheph's family without her husband. Why hadn't she shown up on Adaliah's doorstep?

Brielle reached for a clean cloth with which to wipe her cup, and in doing so revealed one possible answer. Her tunic pulled snug across her round belly. Tanytha might wish to avoid the constant reminder of her own empty womb.

A swell of compassion took Adaliah by surprise. What would her life have been like if she had not been able to give birth? What would her life be like now without Danel? The question didn't bear considering.

"Tonight, when the men come home, I will send Danel to Tanytha with an invitation to join us for a meal."

Brielle looked startled. "Are you sure that's wise?"

Her gaze slid to the grain jar, which Elijah's God continued to fill every morning. When Elijah's true name was discovered, Adaliah had confided the miracle. From that time forward, Brielle refused to touch the jar or the jug that contained Yahweh's oil, claiming them to be holy objects and therefore reserved for the woman to whom the promise had been made.

Adaliah made no answer. No, she wasn't sure the invitation was wise. But she knew in her heart that it was necessary. Whether for Tanytha or for herself, she could not guess.

She put action to words that evening and sent Danel with the invitation. Though Tanytha did not give Danel an answer, Adaliah knew the next morning to put another cushion around their mat. When she uncovered the grain jar, she found it completely full.

Tanytha arrived to share their meal that night and every night after. That she had sunken into despondency in Resheph's absence was apparent to everyone. She rarely spoke, and never when the men were present. When Elijah—who was always referred to as Johanan—gave the nightly thanks to Yahweh for His abundant blessings, she kept her eyes lowered. Once Adaliah saw her fingering a cake of bread, her expression pensive, but she made no mention of the seemingly endless supply of grain. Adaliah gave up trying to draw her out of her morose mood after her first few attempts were quietly but firmly rebuffed.

Brielle refused to be deterred. She confided to Adaliah that Tanytha's continued silence acted like a thorn to her heart.

"Something is bothering her deeply," Brielle insisted. "It isn't normal to stay so quiet for so long."

Adaliah had laughed at the observation. "It would definitely be unusual for *you* to stay quiet that long."

Within a few nights, Tanytha began to respond to Brielle's persistent attempts to draw her into conversation. Indeed, it was difficult not to talk while being peppered with a never-ending stream of questions, enough to rival even Danel's endless curiosity.

On the day the men's work on the boat was finished, Adaliah planned a special meal to celebrate. Tanytha arrived earlier than normal to help with the preparations.

Brielle sat cross-legged on the floor, grinding dried herbs she'd brought with her from Kinneret. "Tell me, Tanni, what spices did your mother use when she cooked fish?"

Tanytha, who was drizzling water on a bowl of dried apples, looked up in surprise. "What did you call me?"

Adaliah hid a smile, while Brielle's cheeks turned pink.

"Tanni." She lifted a dismissive shoulder. "My family does that with people we like. So Adaliah became Addie, and Danel is Dani." She giggled. "I tried to call Eban Ebbie once, but he didn't react well."

To Adaliah's utter shock, Tanytha smiled. "What do they call you?"

"Bree." Her gaze went distant. "My sister sometimes calls me Ellie, but mostly I'm Bree."

"Well, *Bree*," Tanytha replied, her smile deepening, "my mother favored garlic for nearly everything."

By sheer force of will alone, Adaliah managed to keep her jaw from dropping.

At the conclusion of that night's meal, Shemen made an announcement. "Tomorrow I set sail for Sidon."

Danel perked upright. "Can I go with you?"

Adaliah was saved from voicing her protest when Shemen shook his head. "You must stay here and help Eban with the workshop."

A stubborn expression settled on the child's face, which reminded Adaliah strongly of his father. "Johanan can help with that."

"Ah, but I am going with Shemen," Elijah said.

Adaliah twisted on her cushion to look him full in the face. "You are?"

The news sent a flood of worries rushing through her. Was Elijah planning to leave permanently? If he did, would Yahweh keep his promise to provide her with grain and oil until the rains fell?

The prophet dipped his head. "I have a desire to see Sidon, the birthplace of Ahab's wife."

His expression hardened when he mentioned the queen, and Adaliah tossed a glance at Tanytha to see if she noticed. But the woman was lost in her own thoughts, her eyes unfocused.

"How long will you be gone?" Adaliah asked.

Shemen answered. "Only a few days. One day to sail north, a day to settle the payment, and two to return."

Eban launched into a description of the work he and Danel would accomplish while they were gone, a clear attempt to distract the boy from a sulk at being left behind. Adaliah couldn't finish her meal, but as soon as the others did, she pulled Elijah off to one side.

"What will happen when you leave?" she whispered. "Will the grain run out while you're gone?"

The prophet held her gaze for so long she thought he might not answer.

"Why do you still doubt Him?" he asked finally. "Have you not realized that the Lord my God's provision is as much for you and the boy as for me?"

Shame rose up in her, so strong she could not hold his gaze. That Elijah's God would deign to notice her, a sinful woman who had caused the death of not one but *two* people, was not to be considered.

Her chin dropped to her chest. "Your God can have no regard for one such as I."

With a finger under her chin, Elijah lifted her head. "My God, who knows all things, sent me here. He chose your house for a reason." He dipped his head and forced her to meet his gaze. "He chose you."

He left her standing at the bottom of the stairs. She stared at the narrow door to his bedchamber long after he shut it behind him. Though she had no faith in Yahweh's concern for a sinful woman such as herself, how could she not draw confidence from Elijah's words?

# CHAPTER TWENTY-FOUR

The day after Elijah and Shemen boarded the boat and sailed for Sidon, Danel refused to accompany Eban to the workshop. Claiming pain in his head, he remained on his pallet through the morning meal.

Adaliah brought a tray with water and bread into the bedchamber and set it on the floor beside him. She sank to her knees and studied his sleeping form. Fine veins traced across his eyelids, and his nose was straight and almost dainty, like hers. As a baby his lips had fascinated her, the way they pursed when he slumbered, as though kissing a princess in his dreams. Though his face had lost much of the infant roundness, his lips still moved expressively.

His eyes fluttered open, and he fixed her with a sleepy gaze.

"I've brought you something to drink," she said quietly.

He sat up, wincing as he did. "My head hurts, Imma."

She placed a hand on the smooth forehead, which was damp but not feverish. "Drink some water," she told him, and handed him the cup.

When he had taken a few sips, he gave it back to her.

"Good." She smiled tenderly. "Now eat a bite of bread."

But he shook his head. "I'm not hungry."

He lay back down and rolled onto his side away from her. She stayed there until his breathing became slow and even. When she crept from the room, she left the tray.

Eban and Brielle waited for her in the main living chamber.

"Is he sick or merely moping because Shemen and Johanan left without him?" Eban asked.

Adaliah cast a concerned look at the closed curtain. "It isn't like Danel to mope. But there is no fever."

"My younger brothers and sisters often complain of odd aches and ailments, and by the next day they're fine." Brielle placed a comforting hand on Adaliah's arm. "Let him rest, and I'm sure he'll feel better by tonight."

But he did not.

When Tanytha arrived for the evening meal, Danel had not yet risen from his pallet. Whenever Adaliah looked in on him, several times throughout the day, he continued to complain of a pounding in his head. When she threw open the curtains to let fresh air and sunlight flood the room, he cried out in pain and covered his eyes.

Tanytha received the news with more concern than Adaliah expected, since she had never exhibited the slightest care for her half brother.

"Have you examined his skin for a pox?" she asked, deep furrows on her brow.

Throughout the day Adaliah's worry had swelled into a deep, gnawing fear. In his entire life Danel had never been sick, not even with the many minor maladies that affected most babies.

"N-no," she told Tanytha. "I've let him sleep."

"We must check him."

Without waiting for a response, Tanytha swept the curtain aside and entered the bedchamber. With a quick glance at each other, Brielle and Adaliah hurried after her.

Danel lay prone and unmoving, his eyes closed. Adaliah's heart stuttered to see him so still, as though he were laid out on a funeral pyre. Were it not for the slight rise of his chest, she would have feared he was dead.

Tanytha knelt beside the child's pallet. With a touch more tender than Adaliah would have thought her capable, she rested her hand on his forehead. His eyes fluttered open, though his gaze remained unfocused.

"Shhh," Tanytha whispered. "I'll only be a moment. I want to check your skin."

She ran her fingers around both sides of his neck and down his arms and legs. With a quick gesture she enlisted Adaliah and Brielle to help her remove his tunic, crooning in a low, comforting voice when he cried out in pain from being moved. She examined every inch of his body, her expression growing more concerned with every passing minute.

When they settled his tunic back around him and laid him once again on the pallet, he lapsed into sleep. Tanytha rose and stood over him, staring down with an unreadable expression. Gesturing to Adaliah and Brielle to follow her, she slipped out of the bedchamber.

"There is no sign of a rash, and he has no fever," she told them.

"That's good, isn't it?" Brielle asked.

Worry still lay heavy on Tanytha's features. "There are treatments for various kinds of pox, ointments and the like."

"You suspect something." Adaliah wrapped her arms around her middle. "What is it?"

Tanytha hesitated, her lower lip caught between her teeth. "When I was a girl, I had a cousin, the son of my abba's sister."

A sister? Why had Itthobaal never mentioned having family?

"I was only ten when he got sick, but I remember how worried everyone was. He had no fever, no rash, only a terrible pain in his head." She held Adaliah's gaze. "He died before the healers could figure out how to cure him."

A rising darkness threatened to smother Adaliah. A sob escaped her lips, and she squeezed her arms around her waist. Brielle rushed to her side and wrapped her in an embrace.

"You must call the healer," Tanytha told her.

"I—" Adaliah shook her head in an attempt to clear her thoughts.

Brielle tightened her arms. "We must pray to the Lord."

Tanytha cast her an impatient look. "What good will prayers alone do? The priests at the Eshmoun temple are trained in the healing arts."

"Tanni, Yahweh is more powerful than any priest." Brielle implored her to listen. "You just said the healer was not able to save your cousin. What makes you think he can help Danel?"

Their voices pressed in on Adaliah, whose thoughts whipped at a frenzied rate. If anything happened to Danel, her life would be over. She covered her ears and shook her head, trying to clear her mind. Elijah's God had provided for them these past months. Didn't that prove that He cared? If not for her, at least for the precious child in the next room?

But Yahweh was not here, nor was His prophet.

Neither were the healers of Eshmoun, but at least they were only a few hours' journey northeast of Zarephath.

"The healers will bring the sacred waters of Eshmoun," Tanytha insisted.

Brielle drew up stiffly. "Ask your father's sister if the sacred waters helped her son."

"I can't." Tanytha's gaze rested on Adaliah. "After my cousin's death, his mother took her own life."

Adaliah squeezed her eyes shut. How well she understood the grief of a mother whose child the gods had ripped from her arms. That grief loomed over her now, ready to crash in upon her if Danel's life left his body.

That could not happen. Not to her son.

She opened her eyes and stepped away from Brielle to hold herself upright.

"Call the healers," she told Tanytha.

The healer arrived with the sun the next morning in the company of Fayez and a half-dozen priests. Bleary-eyed from a sleepless night at Danel's side, Adaliah let them in. Tanytha, who along with Brielle had maintained a silent vigil in the courtyard from sundown until dawn, set about assembling a meal. Adaliah noted numbly that she moved about the cooking area with an easy familiarity.

*If anything happens to Danel, the house will be hers once again. I won't live here without him.*

Morose thoughts like that one had plagued her throughout the long hours.

Adorned in the elaborate robes of his position, Fayez looked like a peacock perched next to a sparrow. The healer from the Eshmoun temple wore a dingy gray robe with a braided rope looped around his waist in place of a girdle. His head was bare, and his hair hung in unkempt locks round his shoulders. Had she not been held captive by despair, Adaliah would have laughed at Brielle's expression when the man swept past her. He pushed her aside, the other priests trailing single file behind him, and hovered above Danel's pallet. Fayez's sycophants arrayed themselves around the room.

"Addie, come and eat something." Brielle tugged gently on her arm.

Adaliah shook her off, her gaze fixed on her son's face. His features crumpled and he whimpered as he had done much of the night, pain intruding on his sleep. If, indeed, he did sleep. Between bouts of moaning, he lay as still as a corpse, drowning in a state that looked more like death than slumber.

Fayez opened a bundle and spread the contents out on the floor beside the pallet while the healer, whose gaze was fastened on Danel, began a low, guttural chant in a language that Adaliah didn't recognize. The throaty sound sent chills racing up her arms. The other priests joined in, though each seemed to be saying something different, none of it discernible. Brielle gave a violent shudder and, with a worried look at Adaliah, fled from the room.

The priests laid candles out in a circle around the pallet and then lit each one. Statues were placed around the room, of Baal and Astarte and especially of Eshmoun, the god of the healing arts. Someone produced a brazier, and soon the cloying scent of incense filled the bedchamber. Tears stung Adaliah's eyes, and the chanting continued.

Adaliah retreated into a corner and waited.

A day passed without notice, and then a night, and still the healer's chant droned on. His voice grew hoarse and even raspier. Adaliah was vaguely aware that priests came and went, but her world shrank to the confines of the bedchamber and Danel's frail form and the ever-present smell of the smoke that filled her lungs. Twice Tanytha brought food and set it beside her, only to return later and take the untouched tray away.

And then the chanting fell silent.

Adaliah's eyes flew open. She hadn't even been aware that she slept until silence crashed into her soul and thrust her to her feet. Fear swelled into her throat and threatened to choke her. The healer had also risen, and arched his back, his arms thrown wide. He looked at Fayez and, with a slight shake of his head, left the room.

She flew to the pallet and dropped to her knees. "Is he..." She couldn't ask the question.

Fayez stood beside her while the priests gathered their candles and their idols and packed them away in bundles.

"Not yet," the chief priest told her.

"No." She shook her head, watching the slight rise and fall of Danel's chest. "My son is still alive. Make the healer come back."

"Adaliah." Fayez placed a hand on her head. "The gods have spoken. Your son will rest with his father before another day passes."

"No!" The word tore from her throat on a shriek, and she leaped to her feet. She thrust her face into the priest's. "Your gods can't have him. I won't let them take him."

"Calm yourself, woman." His tone held an unmistakable chill.

"Get out!" She placed her hands on his chest and shoved with all her might. "Go back to your bloodthirsty gods of stone and clay, and never return."

Caught unawares, Fayez stumbled backward. He nearly fell but regained his balance. With a tug to straighten his robe, he flicked his fingers across his chest as if to brush away the stain of her touch. Without a word, he left.

Alone with Danel, Adaliah crumpled to the floor.

"Please," she whispered. "Please don't die."

Brielle and Tanytha stayed by Adaliah's side to keep watch while Danel's life ebbed from his body. Through the long hours while the healer and the priests worked over him, he had barely moved. But at the end, his body labored and his lungs wheezed in their effort to draw breath. Adaliah's sobs almost drowned out the sound of his final cry.

And then he lay still.

Adaliah stroked his hair away from his forehead, her tears falling freely. He looked so small, so frail. Her baby.

"Addie." Brielle put her arms around her and hugged. "It's over."

"I—" Adaliah glanced around, at the empty corners of the room. Her brain felt numb, her thoughts distant, as though they belonged to someone else. "I must wash him and get the spices for his burial." She shook her head. "What spices should I get? I—I don't know. And where will I get them?"

"Don't worry about that now." Tanytha bent close and rested her forehead against Adaliah's. "We'll take care of those things later."

Tanytha? What was she doing here? Tanytha hated her, didn't she? But if that were so, why were there tears flowing down her face to mix with Adaliah's own?

"Come." Brielle rose and pulled her to her feet. "Leave him in peace for a little while. Come outside and eat something."

Though her stomach threatened to revolt at the mere mention of food, Adaliah let herself be led from the bedchamber. The numbness in her mind seeped into her limbs, and she leaned heavily on the women who held her up.

Until she rounded the corner into the courtyard.

The ugly statue of Baal leered at her from its corner. Its sightless eyes held a mocking glare that pierced through the depths of her grief. Fayez's words resounded in her brain. *"The gods have spoken."* Rage, hot and fiery, engulfed her, and she shook off her friends' hands. She rushed forward and grabbed the heavy stick she used to stoke the cook fire then raced across the courtyard. Screaming her fury, she swung at the idol. A crack appeared in its clay neck, and she swung again. And again. And again, until the head landed with a thud on the ground. Then she pounded it, over and over, shattering it into a million pieces, like her soul had done when her son—

"Adaliah."

A man's gentle voice broke through the storm. She whirled to find Elijah watching her, with Shemen and Eban standing behind him. Dust from the road still clung to their sandals, the hems of their robes. The prophet's eyes held an ocean of grief, and at the sight of tears streaming down his face, her anger melted like mountain snow in the valley sunshine. The stick fell from her hand. She closed the distance between them and collapsed on his shoulder.

"What do you have against me, man of God?" she sobbed. "If you had stayed away, we would have died together, my son and I. Now I am alone." Her voice broke on the word. "Did you come here to remind me of my sin and kill my son?"

The shoulder beneath her cheek heaved with Elijah's weeping. He held her in a close embrace for a moment, and then pushed her gently back.

"Give me your son," he said.

# CHAPTER TWENTY-FIVE

Elijah cradled Danel's body close to his chest as he ascended the stairs. The sound of Adaliah's mournful crooning and Brielle's soft words of comfort followed him.

*"Did you come here to remind me of my sin and kill my son?"*

Adaliah's words resounded in his mind and tore through his heart.

In the room he had begun to think of as his, Elijah laid the child on his own pallet. He stood above him, gazing down into the face he had come to love. Months ago, when Elijah hid in the Kerith Ravine, the Lord had revealed that he would never have a son of his own. The thought did not disturb him overmuch. When he accepted the call to dedicate his life to Yahweh's service, he knew that service would leave no room for earthly relationships.

He knelt on the mat and laid a hand on Danel's head. How could he not love this child, with his ever-curious delight in learning? A fresh wave of sorrow welled up in Elijah, and his eyes blurred with tears.

"Oh Lord my God," he whispered, "is it not enough that my life is in jeopardy for Your cause, and I must stay hidden away? Have You brought tragedy also on this widow to whom You sent me, by causing her son to die? You know me, Lord, that I could not love a son of my own body any more than I love this boy."

Already Danel's flesh had begun to cool as the chill of death settled over him. If only Elijah could infuse this cold body with his own life, he would gladly do so. He lay down on the pallet and stretched himself out on the child, willing warmth into the unresponsive body, but the effort was useless. He may be a prophet whose word could stop the rain from falling on an entire land, but he could not restore warmth to dead flesh.

Rising, Elijah then paced to the window and gazed down into the courtyard. Adaliah knelt in a huddle on the dirt below him, Brielle holding her as she rocked and Tanytha standing nearby looking helpless. Elijah knew the feeling. From the time of Adam's fall from grace, death was inevitable. No mortal ever born could hope to defeat the judgment of their righteous God on sinful man.

Elijah returned to the pallet and stroked Danel's cheek.

"If I could hide you away so death could not find you, I would," he whispered.

Grief called to him from a dark pit and threatened to pull him in. He lay down and stretched out again on the child, covering him completely. He had no words, but his soul lay bare to his ever-present Lord.

Sound ceased.

Elijah stilled, his spirit calmed by an Eternal Hand.

A vibrant hush seeped into the room. The air seemed to vibrate with an energy that Elijah felt in the deepest part of his spirit. He had spent enough time serving the Lord that he recognized the divine Presence, but never had he felt such vitality, such intensity. He rose onto his knees beside the pallet.

Tears gone in the face of the power that vibrated through-out every fiber of his being, Elijah threw his head back and his arms wide. "Oh Lord my God, I trust You. What would You have me do?"

Moving with an instinct that had no words, Elijah stretched himself out on the pallet a third time. He placed his forehead against Danel's and pressed his nose, his mouth, his chin to the child's. Through the fabric of his tunic he felt the outline of the boy's chest, his thin arms, his legs. Elijah breathed out, his breath a long, warm exhale against Danel's lips.

Then he got up. On his knees again, he placed both hands on the body. Words flowed through his mouth from a Source deep inside. He shouted them toward the heavens with all the strength he could muster.

"Lord my God, let this boy's life return to him!"

Elijah's shout pierced through the cloud of grief that filled Adaliah's entire being. Though she thought there would never be an end to her tears, they dried at the sound of the prophet's voice.

A noise like a mighty wind reverberated throughout the courtyard. The others drew close around her, every eye turned upward.

The door to the upstairs room opened, and the prophet appeared holding Danel in his arms. He hugged the boy tight to his chest as he descended the stairway. Adaliah could not look away from his eyes, which blazed like a dark fire.

"Look," he told her in a husky voice when he reached the bottom step. Tears streamed down the prophet's face. "Your son is alive!"

Danel turned in the prophet's arms to bestow his beloved smile on her. Adaliah covered her mouth with her hands, barely daring to breathe. Shemen let out an exclamation. Beside her Brielle gasped and wavered on her feet. Eban stepped close and held her up, his gaze also fixed on the pair standing at the foot of the stairway. Tanytha gave a small scream and Adaliah was dimly aware that she fled, disappearing through the door and into the street. But she couldn't think about that, for one thought alone consumed her.

*My son is alive.*

Elijah set Danel gently on the ground, and the child ran toward her. Without thinking, Adaliah scooped him into her arms and pulled him tight to her chest, breathing in his sweet scent and relishing the smooth cheek pressed against hers.

Her mind grasped for something to hold on to, something to make sense of the living, breathing boy in her arms. Elijah was right. There truly was no God but Yahweh. No statue of Baal could bring the dead to life.

And if Elijah's words concerning his God were right, then maybe the other things he told her were true as well.

Holding Danel close, she met the prophet's eye over her child's precious head. "Now I know that you are a man of God, and that the word of the Lord from your mouth is the truth."

# CHAPTER TWENTY-SIX

In the aftermath of the most powerful miracle the world had ever seen, Elijah spent three days in prayer. Adaliah sometimes glimpsed him late at night, pacing across the roof, his hands raised to the heavens. On the fourth day, he descended the stairs and took his place around the meal tray as though nothing unusual had happened, as though his God returned life to cold corpses every day of the week.

Following Elijah's example, life returned to normal. Adaliah rose in the morning, ground Yahweh's grain, and made bread for His prophet as she had since Elijah arrived. Shemen and Eban focused their efforts on readying the pottery shop for use. Danel, who seemed unaffected by his ordeal, accompanied the men each day and peppered them with an endless stream of questions. Brielle's belly seemed to grow bigger each night.

And yet, at times throughout the day the realization of Yahweh's incredible power struck Adaliah afresh. She would stop whatever chore she was engaged in, lift her eyes to the endless blue heavens, and whisper a heartfelt, "Thank You."

News of the miracle seeped through the village, though a much-tempered version of the truth.

"The chief priest claims that the god Eshmoun healed Dani," Brielle told them when she returned from the well one morning.

The faces around the courtyard registered varying degrees of outrage.

But Elijah merely laughed. "Let them claim what they will. The Lord my God is not concerned with the false claims of pagans."

Tanytha did not return. A week passed with no sign of her, though Adaliah placed an empty cushion at every meal.

"I'm worried about Tanni," Brielle said one morning after the men had left for the shop. "Keprea told me she tried to call on her a few days ago, but Resheph's mother turned her away."

Adaliah turned from her worktable. "Are they keeping Tanytha hidden away against her wishes?"

Brielle looked troubled. "That was Keprea's concern, and she told them she would not leave their house until she saw her friend." Brielle grinned. "She is a force to be reckoned with when she wants to be."

"I'm sure she is," Adaliah replied dryly. How well she remembered being the object of Keprea's sharp tongue.

"But Farah shut the door in her face and left her standing on the street."

As Tanytha's absence continued, Adaliah had spent much time wondering about the reason. The day of the miracle, Tanytha had no doubt been as stunned as everyone else. Had she closed herself away to wonder at the display of Yahweh's incredible power after the failure of the healer she had insisted on calling? Or was she wrestling with disappointment that "her" house had once again been snatched from her grasp?

Brielle wiped a bowl with a damp cloth, set it on the storage shelf, and then rested a hand atop her stomach. "I think I should go. Maybe they will let me see her."

If Tanytha and the other women of Resheph's family did not respond to Keprea's forceful insistence, then perhaps Brielle's cheerful nature would charm them.

"Would you like to go with me?" Brielle asked.

"No," she answered quickly and then shook her head. "You will have a better reception without me. But here"—she wrapped a stack of bread cakes left from their meal in cloth and extended the bundle—"maybe a gift will give you favor in their eyes."

Brielle took the bread and left, but returned an hour later looking sad.

"She wouldn't see me." She slid onto the stool. "I heard her with my own ears speaking from behind the door to her bedchamber. 'Tell her to go away,' she said." She sat lost in thought for a moment and then added, "Resheph's mother thanks you for the bread."

Adaliah nodded absently, her thoughts on Tanytha. Perhaps she needed time to come to terms with the miracle. They had all been changed by what they'd seen, but Tanytha was the one with a strongly held belief in the gods she had acknowledged since childhood. Perhaps she struggled with the loss of her faith and the realization that Yahweh was the only real God.

"Lord God, show her the way of truth."

She didn't realize she'd spoken the prayer aloud until Brielle grinned at her and said, "Amen."

The next morning Brielle burst into the house, her cheeks flushed and her breath coming in heaves. Once inside, she covered her face with her hands and sobbed.

Eban, who was readying his tools for the day's work, hurried to her side. "What's wrong? Is it the baby?"

She shook her head and pressed into her husband's shoulders. "Something terrible has happened." His tunic muffled her voice. "Poor Tanni."

Adaliah dropped the bowl she held. "What's wrong with Tanytha?"

"Oh Addie." Brielle pulled away from Eban to face her. "There was an accident at sea. High winds or something like that. The boat Resheph was on capsized." Tears streamed down Brielles's face. "He's dead. Drowned, along with half of the crew."

A wave of shock so strong it nearly buckled her knees struck Adaliah, and she grasped at the worktable for support. Resheph, dead? And Tanytha already suffering the loss of her father, and perhaps the loss of her faith. Now she too was a widow. Another widow of Zarephath, and living in a house where she was not welcome.

Adaliah straightened. "I must go to her."

Nodding, Brielle left the circle of Eban's arms and bustled to the worktable. "We'll take some bread, and maybe some of the dried pomegranates I brought from home."

Adaliah stopped her with a raised hand. "I need to go alone."

She thought the young woman might protest, but after a searching glance, she accepted the statement with a nod.

Adaliah grabbed her cloak from its peg on the way out. The air still held a morning chill, and she pulled the garment close around her neck as she hurried through the streets. The village had begun to stir to life, but she ignored those she passed, while her thoughts poured in a constant stream toward the heavens.

*Oh Lord my God, what comfort can I offer a woman who has lost everything? Give me the right words.*

She followed the sounds of grief through the streets, louder as she neared the house. Already a small group of women crowded around the door, their keening wails rising in a heartbreaking chorus. Adaliah wound her way through them, rapped on the door, and didn't wait for it to be opened.

Inside, she found Resheph's family in full mourning. Ashes covered his father's head and he rocked back and forth, moaning. Resheph's mother huddled on the floor, surrounded by her grandchildren, whose bewildered expressions touched Adaliah's heart. She glanced around the courtyard but saw no sign of Tanytha.

Farah caught sight of her and approached with a hard glint in her eye.

Before she could speak, Adaliah stood tall and spoke in a tone that demanded an answer. "Where is Tanytha?"

Farah's eyebrows rose in surprise. She spoke no words, only pointed out a door to one of the rooftop rooms. Without waiting for an invitation, Adaliah marched past the grieving family and up the stairs.

Inside she found Tanytha sitting cross-legged in the far corner, her gaze distant. She did not look up when Adaliah entered and closed the door behind her.

Adaliah crossed the room and lowered herself to the floor beside Tanytha. She grasped about for something to say, some word of comfort she could give, but nothing seemed appropriate. Instead, she merely sat and waited.

Tanytha broke the silence. "I can't cry. I should cry for my husband, but I have no tears."

"They will come in time," Adaliah said.

But Tanytha shook her head. "I've already shed all the tears I ever will for that man." She almost spat the last two words.

Adaliah gave her a sharp look. "What do you mean?"

For a long time she thought Tanytha would not answer. But then she got to her feet. Adaliah remained where she was while Tanytha crossed the room and opened a chest near the door. She rummaged inside for something. When she turned, Adaliah gasped.

Tanytha held Itthobaal's money chest.

"I found it after Resheph left on the sea voyage." She returned to sit beside Adaliah and placed the chest on the floor in front of them. After removing the pegs from the latches, she lifted the lid. The chest was empty.

"He took my abba's money, but that's not all." Tanytha picked up the chest and turned it in her hands to show Adaliah all sides. "It is not singed, and there is no smell of smoke."

Her meaning struck Adaliah, who sucked in a quick breath. "The chest was taken before the fire broke out."

Tanytha turned her head and, for the first time, held Adaliah's gaze. "I think Resheph killed Abba and then stole his money."

"No," Adaliah said softly. "He was trapped beneath a heavy shelf and could not escape the fire."

"And how did the shelf fall? I used to climb on that shelf as a child. It was far too sturdy to fall on its own." Tanytha's lips twisted in an effort to master a sudden sob. "And how did the fire start?"

"Lamp oil." The scent lingered in her memory.

"A leaking lamp would not lose enough oil to cause a fire that devastating," Tanytha said. "You yourself said the floor was covered in burning oil."

"Yes, but…" She fell silent. Another memory surged, one she had not yet considered. "Itthobaal was injured. He was bleeding here." She touched her fingers to her temple. "But the shelf covered his chest. It couldn't have fallen on his head."

"He killed my abba," Tanytha repeated, her voice tortured. "He hit him on the head and then pulled the shelf over to trap him, and then he poured lamp oil across the floor and set it on fire, all while your son slept in the storage room."

Adaliah had no trouble picturing the scene as Tanytha described it. "But why? They got along well together."

"He wanted Abba's business, but Abba refused. He said the kiln and the shop would go to Danel." She winced as she spoke the name. "I asked Resheph after I learned he tried to buy the kiln from you, and he told me about talking to Abba." She paused. "There's more. Resheph knew how badly I wanted the house." Tears welled in the eyes Tanytha lifted to hers. "He killed my abba so I could have your house. Do you see what that means? I am the reason Abba died. Not you."

A week before, the confession would have been a soothing balm on Adaliah's guilt. But since the miracle, that shame no longer burned in her as it had before. How could it, when the Lord God, the Master of life and death, loved her enough to restore her son to her?

"You are not responsible," she told Tanytha. "You must put this behind you. It's over."

"No." Tanytha shook her head. "It will never be over, because..." She spread her hands across her belly. "I am with child."

A cry of joy burst from Adaliah, and she threw her arms around Tanytha.

"Don't you understand?" Tanytha sobbed in her ear. "I am carrying the child of the man who murdered my abba."

"Listen to me." Adaliah grasped her arms and forced her to meet her gaze. "The child in your womb is innocent of any wrongdoing by his father, or by anyone else. He is a blessing, a gift. This child is *yours,* and believe me, he will be the source of your greatest joy." She gave way to a wide grin. "I can hardly wait to meet him."

An answering smile lifted the corners of Tanytha's lips. "What if he is a she?"

"Then her grandmother Adaliah will teach her to make pots." She shrugged. "As soon as she learns how herself. Now come on. Let's gather your things."

Adaliah rose and started across the room.

"Where are we going?" Tanytha asked.

"Home, of course." Adaliah took a tunic from a peg on the wall and began folding it while she gave Tanytha a look that brooked no argument. "*We* are going home."

# EPILOGUE

*Three Years Later*

I wish I could go with you," Danel told Elijah. He cast a sulky glance over his shoulder at Adaliah. "I am old enough."

She leaned against the doorframe to the upstairs room she would always consider as belonging to the prophet of the drought, watching as he stowed his few belongings in the new pack she had stitched for him, since the one he'd arrived with three years earlier had long since fallen to shreds.

Elijah smiled at the boy but said nothing.

"I would tell that king a thing or two." Danel scowled, an expression that so reminded Adaliah of her deceased husband that she suppressed a shiver.

"That is one reason you may not go." The prophet gave him a sympathetic look. "The Lord my God trusts me to speak only the words He gives me, not the ones I would choose if the decision were mine."

"May I go if I promise not to say anything at all?"

Elijah laughed and cast a look at Adaliah. "Then who would take care of your imma?"

Danel answered with no hesitation. "Eban or Shemen."

"Ah, but they have their wives and their children to look after." Elijah folded the top over his pack and slung the long strap over his shoulder. "Tell me the seventh commandment."

Though Adaliah could scarcely believe it, her baby was now seven years old and could recite much of the ancient law by rote. He straightened and recited, "Honor your father and your mother, that your days might be long upon the land which the Lord your God gives you."

Elijah laid a hand on his head. "You are all your imma has. How can you honor her if you desert her?"

Danel's lips turned downward, but he nodded. In the next instant he threw his arms around the prophet's waist. Elijah closed his eyes and returned the boy's embrace. Tears blurred Adaliah's vision. Though their household had grown over the past three years, these two enjoyed a special bond that no one else shared. Danel would miss him terribly.

Elijah retrieved his walking stick from the corner. He paused in the doorway and let his gaze sweep the room as though memorizing it. Adaliah and Danel followed him down the stairs, where the rest of the family waited to bid him farewell.

Eban strode forward and clasped his forearm. "May Yahweh bless your travels."

Elijah turned from him to Bree, who stood flanked by her daughters. "Remember, if you need a bed or a meal, my family in Kinneret will shelter you."

"I will remember."

Elijah placed a hand on each of the little girls' heads. They looked up at him with dark eyes—Miri, who looked like a miniature version of her mother, and Ellie, whom Eban claimed to be an image of his sister. He whispered a blessing over each of them and then smiled at Bree. "I think the next one will be a boy."

She placed a hand on her growing belly. "If he is, we will call him"—she flashed a dimple—"Johanan."

The prophet laughed and turned to the next person waiting to bid him farewell.

Tanni opened the sling she wore around her neck to let the prophet bless her infant while Shemen stood at their side holding his two-year-old stepson. With a hand on each boy's head, Elijah repeated his blessing and then smiled at their parents.

"Performing your marriage ceremony is a memory I will cherish," he told them.

Tears shone in Tanni's eyes. "We will never forget you."

Shemen set little Itthie down and pulled Elijah into an embrace. "Go with Yahweh, my friend." He thumped the prophet's back.

"Always, my brother."

When he released Shemen, Elijah placed a hand on Danel's head. The boy wept openly, and Elijah wiped the tears with his thumb. Then he bent and whispered in Danel's ear. Danel stood straighter, his head held high, and nodded.

Elijah turned to Adaliah. "It is time."

Swallowing a lump of tears that had lodged in her throat, she turned to Bree. "After I see him off, I'll come to the shop to check the packing on that shipment to Gaza. The wagon will arrive late this morning to take it to the harbor."

Bree nodded and spoke to her girls. "Miri, Ellie, get your cloaks. We must go to work."

They left the house together, Adaliah and Elijah, and wound through the streets of Zarephath side by side. Memories rose vividly in her mind's eye. Had it truly been three years since she guided the man of God to her home to feed him a cake of bread?

They stepped through the village gate, and Adaliah stopped. "I stood on this very spot when I first saw you."

He smiled. "Fitting that it should also be where you stand when you see the last of me."

"Is it the last?" She searched his face. "Will we never meet again?"

For a moment his gaze went distant, and then he shook his head. "No."

Now tears did fill her eyes. "Bree has Eban, and Tanni has Shemen, but when you are gone, I will have no one."

"You have Danel."

She smiled through her tears. "Thanks to you."

"You and I both know where the credit belongs." He drew a deep breath. "That will always be the biggest honor of my life."

"What did you tell Danel back there to stop his tears?"

Elijah smiled. "I told him to remember that Yahweh restored his life because He has a holy task that no one but Danel can perform, so he must do all he can to be prepared for when the call comes."

Adaliah wiped her eyes with the back of her hand. "I will miss you."

"May I tell you a secret?" The prophet leaned forward and whispered in her ear. "You will not miss me for long. When the drought on this land ends, so will the drought in your heart. You may want to move Danel back into his upstairs room to make way for your bridegroom."

A thrill shot through her, but she pushed it aside. Time enough to ponder the prophecy later. Instead, she rose on her toes and placed a kiss on Elijah's cheek.

"You ended the drought in my heart when you came into my house and brought the Lord our God with you."

When she drew back, he placed his hand on her head. "The Lord bless you, and keep you, and give you peace."

Adaliah stayed at the gate, watching as his figure receded into the distance. Dust rose from the dry, thirsty ground with every footstep.

Something touched her cheek. She lifted her hand and brushed a drop of moisture onto her fingertip. Overhead the sun beat down on the earth from a clear blue sky, but Adaliah knew—she *knew*—that soon Yahweh would send the rains and life would spring from the parched land once again. Just as He had brought life to her.

# FACTS BEHIND
## *the Fiction*

❖

# FRIENDLY NEIGHBORS:
# ANCIENT ISRAEL AND LEBANON

When Elijah and, later, Jesus needed a place to refresh and regroup, they retreated to what is now called Lebanon—a narrow stretch of land wedged between the Lebanon Mountain range and the Mediterranean Sea. Known then as Phoenicia, it was a welcome location for Jews.

Phoenicians and Jews had been getting along for at least a thousand years, since the days of King Solomon when Phoenicians helped him build the world's first Jewish temple.

King Hiram of Tyre, a Phoenician seacoast city a few miles south of Zarephath, sold Solomon lumber for the temple: cedar of Lebanon. This was the insect-resistant, rot-resistant wood Phoenician shipbuilders preferred. Hiram's men delivered the massive logs by floating them down the seacoast and then hauling them about 35 miles (50 km) inland to Jerusalem. Hiram even sent artisans, including carpenters, stonecutters, and metalworkers, to help in the construction.

The Jews likely remembered that fondly. Solomon's Temple survived about 600 years, before the invading Babylonians leveled Jerusalem in 586 BC.

In Elijah's day, most Phoenicians didn't call themselves that. Phoenicia was a region

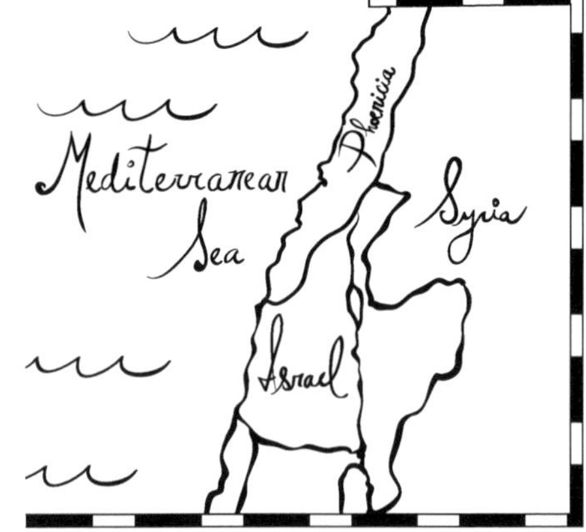

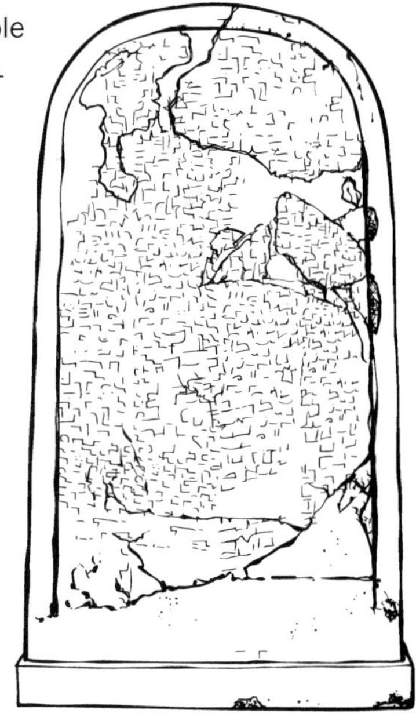

TWO VARIETIES OF MUREX
SEA SNAIL SHELLS

of independent cities. So, if a family lived in the area of Sidon, for example, they were Sidonians. Phoenicia is a name Greeks apparently coined from their word *phoenix.* It means "purple" and "red." It refers to the expensive dye Phoenicians derived from murex sea snails.

Phoenicia covered roughly four thousand square miles (around ten thousand square kilometers). That's almost the size of Connecticut and four times larger than Rhode Island.

# KING AHAB'S FATHER MENTIONED ON A STONE MONUMENT

There aren't many people in the Bible whose names have been found in archaeological discoveries of their time. Ahab's father, King Omri, ruler of the northern Jewish nation of Israel, is one of the few.

A neighboring king, Mesha, ruler of Moabites in what is now Jordan, claimed his kingdom had finally broken free of "the House of Omri." This boast, which Mesha had engraved into a stone monument now preserved as the Moabite Stone, survives as a tribute to Omri's power, which reached beyond his own kingdom.

THE MESHA STONE (AKA MESHA STELE OR MOABITE STONE)

Scholars date the stone text to about 850 BC. That aligns with the time Bible experts say Mesha rebelled against Omri's grandson, who ruled the third and last generation of Omri's dynasty. The Bible says Mesha rallied his soldiers—who were about to lose the battle—by sacrificing his oldest son on the city wall. The Moabites fiercely attacked the Israelites, who were horrified by the sacrifice they witnessed. Israel's army "withdrew and returned to their own land" (2 Kings 3:27 NLT).

# MAKING OLIVE OIL

In Bible times as well as now, handpicked olives required gentle fingers to pick them at harvest time. Too much pressure, and olives release oil, which reduces their value. Oil is what swells pulp into a plump, black olive. Half the weight of pulp in a mature black olive is oil. That oil is the farmer's pay for a year's work.

Olives don't mature until around November, which made them one of the last crops harvested in the Middle East. In the past, growers often built olive presses right beside their olive trees. That way, harvesters didn't have to transport olives on bumpy trails, which could bruise the olives and release their oil.

Ancient growers used two kinds of presses for two different pressings. The first pressing produced the purest oil,

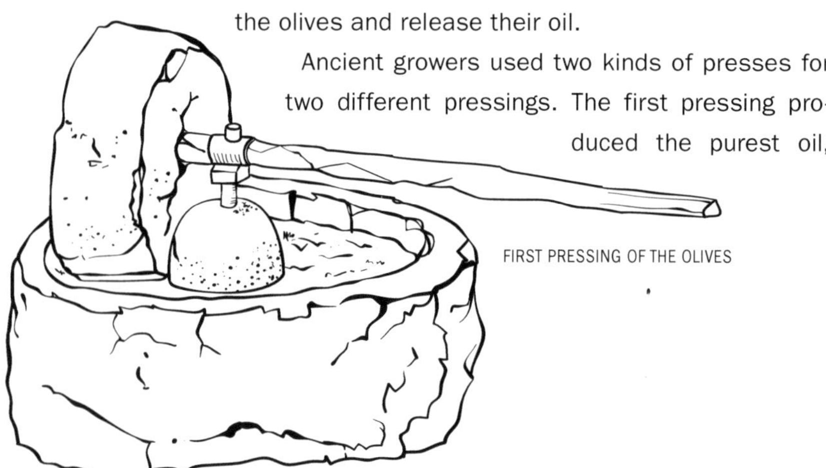
FIRST PRESSING OF THE OLIVES

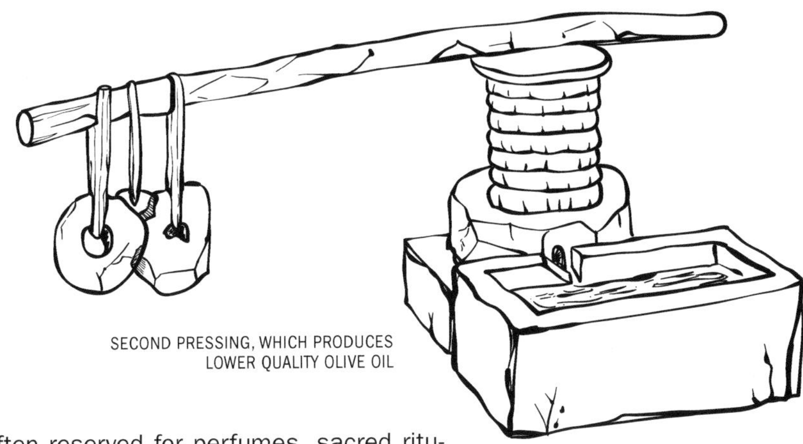



often reserved for perfumes, sacred rituals, and lamps. Harvesters poured the olives
into a large stone basin shaped like a wheel lying on its side and chis-
eled out like a bowl. The press had a rod extending up through a raised
hole in the center. The rod connected to a beam of wood. A crushing
stone was attached to one end of the beam, and this stone rolled over
the olives. At the other end of the beam, an animal or a worker powered
the stone by pushing the beam in a circle around the large basin. Harvesters used wedges and other techniques to position the crushing
stone low enough to squeeze the pulp but high enough to avoid break-
ing olive pits, which would contaminate the virgin oil with sediment.

For a second pressing, harvesters scooped the crushed olives into
woven baskets. They piled several baskets on top of each other in a
stone vat built to collect olive oil drippings. They laid a thick wooden
beam across the top of the baskets. And they slid one end of the beam
into a niche cut into a sturdy wall. On the other end, they tied heavy
rocks. Under the weighted beam, which squeezed the baskets together,
olives released the last of their oil. The heavier the rocks, the more
oil—but the lower the quality of oil, because of increased sediment
from crushed pulp. This is the oil people often used to cook their food.

Even today, the first pressing of olive oil is more highly valued and
thus more expensive.

Elijah is perhaps most famous for the way he left this world—often described as riding a chariot of fire into heaven, though the Bible doesn't describe it quite that way.

In fact, some people reading the story in the Bible might say it seems more likely he got taken up into a tornado during a lightning storm. He and his apprentice, Elisha, were walking east of the Jordan River when "suddenly a chariot of fire appeared, drawn by horses of fire. It drove between the two men, separating them, and Elijah was carried by a whirlwind into heaven" (2 Kings 2:11 NLT).

Some might read "chariots of fire" as a poetic way of describing the lightning that struck between the two men. But many Christians take the story literally, and would note that celestial beings in the Bible are often associated with bright light. For instance, take the angel announcing the Resurrection of Jesus: "His face shone like lightning, and his clothing was as white as snow" (Matthew 28:3 NLT).

ELISHA WATCHING AS ELIJAH IS TAKEN AWAY IN A "CHARIOT OF FIRE."

# MIRACLES OF ELIJAH

- **Drought:** Stopped rain for three and a half years (1 Kings 17:1; Luke 4:25).

- **Fed by birds:** Ate bread and meat delivered by ravens (1 Kings 17:4).

- **Flour, oil:** Produced flour and oil for widow of Zarephath (1 Kings 17:16).

- **Resurrection:** Brought widow's dead son back to life (1 Kings 17:22).

- **Lightning:** Called down lightning to light a water-soaked animal sacrifice (1 Kings 18:38).

- **Rain:** Ended drought (1 Kings 18:45).

- **Prediction:** Correctly predicted end of Ahab's dynasty and family (1 Kings 21:22; 2 Kings 10:6-7).

- **Prediction:** Correctly predicted dogs would eat Jezebel's corpse (1 Kings 21:23; 2 Kings 9:35-36).

- **Prediction:** Correctly predicted King Ahaziah would die of his injury in a fall (2 Kings 1:4, 17).

- **Lightning:** Called down lightning that killed 50 soldiers coming to arrest him (2 Kings 1:10).

- **Lightning:** Called down lightning to 50 more soldiers coming to arrest him (2 Kings 1:12).

- **Stops a river:** Parted the Jordan River and walked across the riverbed (2 Kings 2:8).

- **Prediction:** Correctly predicted Elisha would get a double portion of Elijah's spirit (2 Kings 2:10, 14).

- **Taken away:** Carried away in a whirlwind with a celestial escort (2 Kings 2:11).

Elisha had asked for twice the spirit of his mentor, Elijah. One clue he got his wish: Elisha is credited with twice as many miracles as Elijah, including some of resurrections.

We don't know God's name. All we have is an educated guess.

When Moses asked God what His name was, God first seemed to explain what the name meant: "I AM WHO I AM" (Exodus 3:14 NASB). Many Jewish scholars translate the Hebrew words in that same Bible verse into a future tense: "I WILL BE WHAT I WILL BE."

The next thing God did was to give that explanation a nickname: I AM (or perhaps I WILL BE). "Say this to the people of Israel: I AM has sent me to you" (NLT). That's just a shorter version of the longer explanation. In Hebrew, the word is *Ehyeh* (AY-hyah), short for the full explanation, *Ehyeh-Asher-Ehyeh*.

After God explained His name, He told Moses the name: "Say this to the people of Israel: Yahweh, the God of your ancestors—the God of Abraham, the God of Isaac, and the God of Jacob—has sent me to you. This is my eternal name" (Exodus 3:15 NLT).

## WRITING THE NAME OF GOD

*Yahweh* (YAH-way) is just an educated guess, and here's why:

Jews in ancient times wrote only in consonants—no vowels. It saved space on scrolls. God's name in Hebrew as it appears in the Bible more than 6,000 times is *Yhwh*. Scholars say Moses and others probably passed along the pronunciation by word of mouth. But it was lost somewhere along the way.

Jewish scholars didn't add vowels to their Bible, what Christians call the Old Testament, until a thousand years ago. That's about the time of the Crusades, and more than 2,000 years after the Bible says Moses talked with God.

And so *Yhwh* is the only name we really have.

Imagine if all we knew of Jesus' name was Jss. Would we come up with Jesus? Or would we go with Jesse? Most English Bibles translate God's name as "LORD," with small caps. When we read that word in the Old Testament, we're reading an English substitute for God's name.

Jews offer their own substitute, out of respect for God. When they read YHWH in their Bible, they say *Adonai* (ADD-doe-nigh), which means "my Lord."

HEBREW LETTERS SPELLING OUT YHWH (YAHWEH)

# GOD VS BAAL

Of all the ancient so-called deities who might have competed with God in a thunderbolt-throwing contest—like the one Elijah instigated with Queen Jezebel's prophets (see 1 Kings 18)—Baal was the most likely contender.

He was the god of rainstorms. He shows up in ancient pictures toting what looks like thunderbolt javelins. But Baal was more than the god of rainstorms, which were usually cherished in the dry Middle East. He was god of fertility in families, fields, and flocks. If someone wanted more children, a good harvest, and more livestock, Baal was considered the god to call.

Baal attracted many Jews, especially after the Jews first arrived in Canaan as refugees escaped from Egypt. Likely, they were new and inexperienced farmers, since the Bible describes them as slaves who made mud bricks. Perhaps they saw Canaanites—experienced farmers—growing better harvests. So some Jews decided to worship Baal for a good harvest and God for protection from enemies.

God, not willing to become just another god in the pantheon (see Exodus 34:14), sent prophets like Elijah to warn people about it.

A DEPICTION OF BAAL

## Fiction Author
# VIRGINIA SMITH

Bestselling author **Virginia Smith's** first novel was published in 2006. Since then, she's written more than fifty books that have collected a satisfying number of accolades and awards, including two Holt Medallion Awards of Merit. An avid reader with eclectic tastes in fiction, Ginny writes in a variety of styles, from light-hearted relationship stories to breath-snatching suspense. She and her husband live in the bluegrass state of Kentucky (where the grass is green, not blue) with a feisty Maltese named Max.

## Nonfiction Author
# STEPHEN M. MILLER

**Stephen M. Miller** is an award-winning, best-selling Christian author of easy-reading books about the Bible and Christianity. His books have sold over 1.9 million copies.

Miller lives in the suburbs of Kansas City with his wife, Linda, a registered nurse. They have two married children who live nearby.

# A PERILOUS JOURNEY:
# PHOEBE'S STORY

by Mary DeMuth

*Cenchrea, AD 58*

I cannot." Phoebe sat on a stone bench in her villa's atrium, smoothing her linen *stola* in a vain effort to keep her hands from trembling. For a brief moment, she allowed her gaze to look up at Paul. His piercing scrutiny weakened her resolve to stand firm in her refusal to his request. She bowed her head once more.

"I cannot," she repeated. In the periphery of her vision, she saw the intense man begin to pace. Then he paused and sat on a bench opposite her. His very presence demanded she look at him.

"You're the one I trust, Phoebe." His tone softened when he spoke her name. "And you're the one with means. You're our Esther, raised up for a time such as this."

His earnestness stole her voice in that moment. The weight of his words burdened her heart. True, God had rescued her…

and ruined her. And yet, though He slay her, she would remain wholly committed to the cause of Christ.

Paul, the apostle to the Gentiles, the earnest disciple of Yeshua, stood again. "You remember my words, don't you? About fools?"

She nodded and reached for an earthen cup, slaking her dried throat with clear water. "Yes, yes, of course."

"God doesn't call the clever. He doesn't chase the wise. He looks for the weak. He uses those the world considers foolish to shame the learned. These are the people who bring Him glory, the ones who allow His reputation to shine—to shine like your name, Woman of Light."

He spoke the truth. Her name, Phoebe, meant light. However, until she met Yeshua, her life had been shrouded in a gray fog. She had never quite been able to see things clearly. She chased after success and a high reputation for herself, for her husband, for their endeavors. But even as good fortune upon good fortune graced their household, her heart shrank with each victory. The fog gave way to darkness, and she was left hoping there was more to life than what she'd found. She swallowed the memories that threatened to strangle her. "I am no one, Paul," she said, shaking her head. "There must be someone better equipped to do what you are asking."

Paul paced before the *impluvium* as the sun danced upon the captured rainwater. "Regardless of what you think, I am convinced you are the one the Almighty has called to do this task."

"You forget my gender," Phoebe said.

"There is neither male nor female, Jew nor Greek…" Paul's voice trailed.

"But a widow? Alone in the world? Shunned by all? Who am I that you would ask such a request?" She studied the gold rings on her fingers. "There are some things not even my wealth can buy."

"You call yourself shunned," Paul replied. "And that is true. You have been forsaken by everyone—by father and mother, aunt and uncle, by in-laws and neighbors, by death itself as it ceased your husband's breath. What you say is wholly accurate." Paul paused just long enough to let his words sink in; but when he spoke again, his voice was barely above a whisper. "Have you forgotten the great reversal of the Kingdom of God, Phoebe? That you are dearly loved? A child of the God who created it all? You are a deacon in His church, a wise steward of wealth, a chosen person, a minister of Yeshua, the Christ. You have been bought with a price. And now I ask you to spend yourself for Him."

She sighed then stood to match his gaze. "When you say it that way…"

"I'm not trying to woo you with clever words, Phoebe. I simply ask you to pray and seek His will in the matter, as I have. I'd certainly go myself if I could. This scroll contains my heart, the very words of the Lord for a people in desperate need in Rome. Priscilla and Aquila need these words. The *oikos* needs them. Would you carry them for me? Please?"

Phoebe watched the sun dip beneath the roofline of her inner courtyard. She shivered. "I will pray. This is a decision that must not be made without careful consideration."

Paul dipped his head. "Yes, this involves far more than a journey."

She walked beside him toward the outer portico, where roses had escaped their confines and scrambled up the stone walls, scenting their way.

Now in the street, Paul's eyes moistened. "There will no doubt be danger. I cannot promise otherwise."

"That is not the reason for my reticence," Phoebe said.

"What is it, then?" Paul beckoned her to follow him on the path. The sun fairly danced upon the early evening, casting the world in vibrant light and depth of shadow. They walked in silence while the sun sank lower on the horizon and the shadows grew like trees behind them.

How could she express what was in her heart? This request weighted itself with expectation, and she feared she would dash Paul's hopes. She remembered his letter when he called her body of believers to account, when Marcus slept with his father's wife without shame. Paul had shed holy light not simply upon the fornication but laid blame at the feet of the entire church for not bringing this transgression to the forefront. She had been afraid to call out such darkness herself, reasoning they could move forward, forgetting Marcus's sin, and continue serving their Savior. But Paul spoke of leaven—that even a little yeast of sin permeates the entire dough—and soon Marcus's sin would knead its way through their body of believers. Paul wanted them to be what he called "unleavened bread of sincerity and truth." They were to deliver Marcus to Satan, the adversary, in hopes that he would turn from his incestuous ways. Expelling him meant they would welcome the holiness of God back into their midst. And so they did.

And, miraculously, when they chastised Marcus, he eventually repented, while Paul encouraged them all to welcome him back as a brother—with lovingkindness.

"I may fail you," Phoebe finally managed.

"I am not God. I am not the one to hold you accountable. I am simply asking you to consider my request."

The early evening quieted while birds sang lazy songs, and the air thickened with surprising humidity.

"It is a long journey for a woman alone," she said into the cooling air. "I trust only Trecia to accompany me, but two women traveling alone will be an anomaly in the empire."

Paul laughed then, a full-hearted, rare explosion that seemed to erupt from his lungs. "I would not ask you to make such a journey without a guard, Phoebe. Joses will go with you. He is trustworthy, strong, and capable."

"I do not know him." Fear gripped her heart. However, not in the way one might think. No, she had been a married woman, acquainted with the ways of men. But even now, her father's contorted face still haunted her, his words of wrath and rancor piercing her heart with the same fresh pain as it had then.

When Phoebe had proclaimed the name of Jesus as Lord, her mother's pleas had injured Phoebe's heart. Yet it was her father's unconditional abandonment that strangled her. Her parents' love swiftly terminated at the mention of His Name. Even so, she could not, would not, betray Yeshua. If she thought she knew her father, and he turned his back, what betrayal might a stranger be capable of? Still, she trusted Paul, believed his words. Surely this man he recommended represented his same integrity.

"He will protect you. You must allow him to accompany you." Paul's words wove between them, stringing an air of authority, tinted with fatherly concern.

Phoebe turned. "It will be getting dark soon. I need to get back inside. But let me assure you, I will pray about this endeavor."

Paul returned her to her villa, nodded again in the fading light. "I cannot overemphasize the importance of this request, Phoebe. These words need to find their way into the hearts and minds of the Roman believers. God has shown me as much. And I believe you are the person to bring this about."

She lingered beneath the tangle of roses then sighed as the apostle to the Gentiles ambled back down the path. His eyes strained, she knew, at the darkness. To navigate, he traced his fingers along the stone wall to his right.

"My lady?" Trecia startled her from behind.

Phoebe tried to shed the weight of the conversation, tried to appear lighthearted, carefree. "Yes, Trecia?"

"I have prepared some roasted lamb and dates, and a little cheese. It is time for your evening meal." Trecia motioned Phoebe inside, where her supper had been spread out on a low table.

Phoebe ate in silence, wrangling Paul's words, chewing on them as she swallowed overcooked lamb. When Trecia offered a flat of bread, she instinctively ripped it in half, then remembered the words of Yeshua on the night He was betrayed, as had been recounted by those who reclined with Him. *"Take; eat,"* He had said. *"This is my body, broken for you."*

At this thought, emotion gripped her heart again, torn between fear of what human beings were capable of doing and her incessant longing to please the One who had set her gloriously free from her previous life of idolatry. Though Phoebe ate in silence, Trecia broke the quiet with her own words, chattering on and on about market prices, two lambs she met on the way with black faces, and the new weaving she was attempting to conquer. Words, words, words. While Trecia's words comforted her as the evening slipped into night, it was Paul's words that echoed through her thoughts when sleep eluded her.

*Oh, dear Yeshua, what do You want me to do? I am afraid.*

# A NOTE FROM THE EDITORS

We hope you enjoyed another volume in the Ordinary Women of the Bible series, created by Guideposts. For over seventy-five years, Guideposts, a nonprofit organization, has been driven by a vision of a world filled with hope. We aspire to be the voice of a trusted friend, a friend who makes you feel more hopeful and connected.

By making a purchase from Guideposts, you join our community in touching millions of lives, inspiring them to believe that all things are possible through faith, hope, and prayer. Your continued support allows us to provide uplifting resources to those in need. Whether through our communities, websites, apps, or publications, we inspire our audiences, bring them together, and comfort, uplift, entertain, and guide them. Visit us at guideposts.org to learn more.

We would love to hear from you. Write us at Guideposts, P.O. Box 5815, Harlan, Iowa 51593 or call us at (800) 932-2145. Did you love *The Last Drop of Oil: Adaliah's Story*? Leave a review for this product on guideposts.org/shop. Your feedback helps others in our community find relevant products.

# Find more inspiring stories in these best-loved Guideposts fiction series!

## Mysteries of Lancaster County

Follow the Classen sisters as they unravel clues and uncover hidden secrets in Mysteries of Lancaster County. As you get to know these women and their friends, you'll see how God brings each of them together for a fresh start in life.

## Secrets of Wayfarers Inn

Retired schoolteachers find themselves owners of an old warehouse-turned-inn that is filled with hidden passages, buried secrets, and stunning surprises that will set them on a course to puzzling mysteries from the Underground Railroad.

## Tearoom Mysteries Series

Mix one stately Victorian home, a charming lakeside town in Maine, and two adventurous cousins with a passion for tea and hospitality. Add a large scoop of intriguing mystery, and sprinkle generously with faith, family, and friends, and you have the recipe for *Tearoom Mysteries*.

## Ordinary Women of the Bible

Richly imagined stories—based on facts from the Bible—have all the plot twists and suspense of a great mystery, while bringing you fascinating insights on what it was like to be a woman living in the ancient world.

**To learn more about these books,
visit Guideposts.org/Shop**

Printed in the United States
by Baker & Taylor Publisher Services